ALL-STAR PLAYERS,
ALL-STAR PLAYS . . .

You are there as

Dan Marino, in his second season, throws an amazing 48 touchdown passes and passes for 5,084 yards . . .

John Elway leads his legendary 98-yard touchdown drive in the closing minutes of the AFC title game against Cleveland . . .

Bernie Kosar faces down Doug Flutie in a college classic that is one of the greatest quarterback confrontations of all time . . .

Warren Moon builds his reputation as one of the most feared signal callers in the league.

Here are their stories, on and off the gridiron, in the book that's a *must* on every football fan's list!

GREAT QUARTERBACKS OF THE NFL

GREAT QUARTERBACKS OF THE N.F.L.®

BILL GUTMAN

AN ARCHWAY PAPERBACK
Published by POCKET BOOKS
New York   London   Toronto   Sydney   Tokyo   Singapore

AN ARCHWAY PAPERBACK *ORIGINAL*

An Archway Paperback published by
POCKET BOOKS, a division of Simon & Schuster Inc.
1230 Avenue of the Americas, New York, NY 10020

ISBN: 0-671-79244-X

First Archway Paperback printing September 1993

10 9 8 7 6 5 4 3 2 1

AN ARCHWAY PAPERBACK and colophon are registered
trademarks of Simon & Schuster Inc.

All cover photos by Focus On Sports except: front cover, lower
right by John Biever/*Sports Illustrated;* and back cover, top by
John McDonough/*Sports Illustrated*

Printed in the U.S.A.

Acknowledgments

The author would like to thank the public relations departments of the Buffalo Bills, Miami Dolphins, Denver Broncos, Cleveland Browns, Houston Oilers, and Dallas Cowboys for their help in furnishing background material used in preparation of this book. Also the Sports Information Departments at the University of Miami, University of Pittsburgh, University of Washington, University of California at Los Angeles, and Stanford University.

A special thanks to Vernon J. Biever for providing some of his fine NFL photos taken during a long and distinguished career as the Green Bay Packers' official photographer.

INTRODUCTION

IN THE WORLD OF PROFESSIONAL FOOTBALL, THE quarterback is almost always looked upon as *the* main man. No one watching a big National Football League game today, especially a playoff game, can see it any differently. Sure, a winning team must be well-rounded on both offense and defense. It must also have outstanding players at a number of key positions. But just watch whom the television cameras focus on most during the course of the game. Even if he isn't his team's biggest star, the quarterback is still the focal point of the action and the player who best reflects the emotional ups and downs of his team.

It has been that way ever since a reed-thin Texan named Sammy Baugh came out of Texas Christian University to join the Washington Redskins in 1937. "Slingin' Sam" revolutionized the quarterback position by dominating the game with passing.

Since Baugh, the NFL has seen such strong-armed

luminaries as Sid Luckman, Bob Waterfield, Norm Van Brocklin, Bobby Layne, Otto Graham, John Unitas, Bart Starr, Y. A. Tittle, Sonny Jurgensen, Joe Namath, Fran Tarkenton, Terry Bradshaw, Dan Fouts, Roger Staubach, and Joe Montana. There were others, too, capable of taking a team to victory with their strong throwing arms.

Behind every quarterback is a distinctive personality. Baugh was the strong, silent, tough-as-nails Texan. Layne was the guy who could party half the night and still play with creative winning brilliance. Unitas is still called by some the best ever. Bradshaw had the golden arm, Namath the gimpy knees and shotgun release. Tarkenton was the original "scrambler." Staubach specialized in the last-second comeback, and Joe Montana has made the comeback a fine art. And they all did their thing while being chased, harassed, hit, battered, and bruised.

Today's great quarterbacks possess the same qualities of greatness—incredible athletic ability, toughness, a will to win, individuality, and the desire to get the job done under pressure. To compare them to the quarterbacks who came before is sure to start an argument, but one that can never be settled.

So when you read about Miami's Dan Marino, Buffalo's Jim Kelly, Denver's John Elway, Houston's Warren Moon, Cleveland's Bernie Kosar, and Dallas's Troy Aikman, just enjoy them for who they are. These are six of the very best signal callers of this generation, and all have achieved their present status in different ways and by traveling different roads. *Great Quarterbacks of the NFL* will take you along on the action-packed journeys of these six men.

DAN MARINO

BORN IN PITTSBURGH, AND A HIGH-SCHOOL STAR there, and then an All-American quarterback at the University of Pittsburgh, Dan Marino seemed to be writing "a tale of one city." The proper ending would have had Marino drafted by the Pittsburgh Steelers to continue with a pro career in his hometown.

Even stories with happy endings don't always follow fairy-tale scripts, though. The Steelers did have a chance to draft Marino in 1983, but they passed on him. Instead, the Miami Dolphins picked the 6'4″, 215-pounder with the quick release and rifle arm. It was in Miami, not Pittsburgh, that Marino became an NFL record-setting passer widely acknowledged to be one of the best ever to play the game.

Daniel Constantine Marino, Jr. was born in Pittsburgh on September 15, 1961. His father, Dan Sr., played football in high school but was not a star player and never went to college. The elder Marino was a hard-working man whose life revolved around home and family. The Marinos always had a closeness and loyalty to one another, their neighborhood, and their city.

Dan Sr. and his wife, Veronica, still live in the same neighborhood in Pittsburgh where they raised Dan and his two sisters, Cindi and Debbie.

Young Dan became involved with sports early. He recalls bats, balls, and gloves as being among his principal toys. His father was always ready to play catch with him, and from the first he encouraged his son to enjoy sports and to play for the fun of it.

Dan and his friends would play any sport any chance they had. It was at St. Regis grade school that Dan began to play football. His first coach was none other than his father, and it was Mr. Marino who decided that his son should be the quarterback.

"Dad made me the quarterback because I could throw the ball the best," Dan remembered.

It wasn't long before young Dan began to show star quality, and sports began to take up more and more of his time. When he was nine he was a winner of the local Punt, Pass, and Kick competition.

He remembers some of the street games he and his friends played back then. "We played touch football, street hockey, and games like release the peddler," he said. "And I must have broken about twenty windows at St. Regis playing ball as a kid."

At Catholic Central High School he became a two-sport star, pitching strikes on the diamond and passing for touchdowns on the gridiron. When he wasn't pitching, he was a rangy shortstop with a rifle arm and was always a top hitter. It was hard to tell which was his better sport—he totally enjoyed both of them. By the time he began his senior year in 1978, Dan

4

was one of the biggest high-school stars in the city. But being Saturday's hero didn't change him.

"Dan always had his feet on the ground," said Central's football coach, Rich Erdelyi. "He never was starstruck with himself."

Well over six feet tall and approaching 200 pounds, Dan was a commanding presence who knew how to run a passing offense. In one game he completed 17 of 39 passes. He had an extremely strong arm and, more important, a very quick release. When he saw a receiver open—Boom!—he got the ball there.

Dan became a *Parade* magazine All-American as a senior. He was also named the Most Valuable Player for Western Pennsylvania and was the AAA All-State quarterback. He was one of the top quarterback prospects in the country and the question was whether he would seek collegiate glory in Pittsburgh. Ultimately, he made the final choice by himself.

That choice turned out to be Pittsburgh. The only thing that threatened his decision was his own athletic skills. Shortly after his senior year ended, the Kansas City Royals made him their fourth-round choice in the free-agent baseball draft. They wanted to sign him right then. Dan decided to stick with football.

So it was off to the University of Pittsburgh in the fall of 1979. By then Dan was nearly 6'4" and weighed over 200 pounds, a great size for a college quarterback.

The Pittsburgh Panthers, however, had a fine quarterback returning that fall. He was junior Rick Trocano, an outstanding athlete who was both a solid runner and passer. Trocano opened the season as the starter, but Coach Jackie Sherill said that Marino would see action, especially in passing situations.

Kansas University was Pitt's opponent in the opening game and, sure enough, Dan had a chance to play. He entered midway through the game, and his first collegiate passing attempt was picked off by the Jayhawk defense.

Undaunted, he almost had his second pass intercepted, too. But on his third passing attempt, Marino connected with his receiver for a touchdown! It was a sign of things to come. He completed 5 of 11 passes for 79 yards as Pittsburgh won, 24–0.

Trocano remained the starter for the next five games. Then came Navy, and Coach Sherill decided to go to Marino early. The big freshman came through. Playing with the poise of a seasoned veteran, Dan hit on 22 of 30 passes for 227 yards and a pair of scores. Pittsburgh won easily. After the game Coach Sherill made a tough decision. With Syracuse up next, he named Dan Marino his starting quarterback.

Dan hit 18 of 26 passes for 170 yards and a pair of scores against the Orangemen. A week later he threw for 232 yards against West Virginia, then 272 versus Army, and finally 279 in a 29–14 victory over archrival Penn State. Pitt had a 10-1 record, losing only to North Carolina. They were on their way to meet Arizona in the Fiesta Bowl.

In that one, Dan hit 15 of 29 for 172 yards as the Panthers emerged victorious, topping the Wildcats, 16–10. He finished the season completing 130 of 222 passes for 1,680 yards and 10 scores. His completion percentage was a fine 58.6, and he had just nine tosses picked off. Those numbers made him the 10th-rated passer in the country and tops among freshmen.

Dan was happy about the decision he had made to

6

At the University of Pittsburgh, Dan Marino became one of the most feared passers in the country. With Dan at the helm, the Panthers could strike from anywhere on the field.

(Courtesy University of Pittsburgh)

remain in Pittsburgh. "It's great to be able to play in front of my friends and family," he said. "I've gotten great publicity and I'm still home."

He began his sophomore year with a five-interception, two-touchdown game in the opener. Then Dan really began to heat up. He threw for five scores in the next two games, then had career bests of 282 and 286 yards passing in the two after that, though in the second of those games the Panthers were upset by Florida State, 36–22. But Dan was still playing outstanding football.

Then in the sixth game, against West Virginia, Dan had to leave early with a knee injury. He sat out the next three games. When he returned, he threw for 292 yards with a 20-for-30 performance against Army, but his knee was still troubling him. He played sparingly against Penn State as Pitt won, 14–9, then helped the club top South Carolina in the Gator Bowl, 37–9.

The Panthers had another 11-1 season, with Dan completing 116 of 224 passes for 1,609 yards and 15 touchdowns. He had 14 passes pilfered. When the season ended he underwent surgery on the bad knee. So when the 1981 season rolled around, he was something of a question mark.

But as soon as the schedule began, it was obvious that Dan was healthy, and football fans everywhere knew about it. He put together a totally incredible season. Against Cincinnati he completed 22 of 30 passes for 270 yards and five big touchdowns. A week later he threw for a career-best 346 yards, hitting on 24 of 39 passes and six touchdowns in a 42–28 victory over South Carolina. That made 11 scoring aerials in two games.

He was now setting records nearly every week. After only four games he had 16 TD tosses and had set a new Pittsburgh mark for a single season. The accolades were rolling in.

Bobby Bowden, the coach of Florida State, had this to say: "Marino will dominate college quarterbacks for as long as he's around. . . . He's a great passer, unbelievable. He's a pro quarterback in college, really."

For Army's coach, Ed Cavanaugh, Dan was flat-out number one. "He's the best I've seen at that position in a long time," Cavanaugh said. "Quick delivery, great arm. Our staff watched him in films and I've never seen a staff so unanimous in their praise of one player."

Going into their final contest against Penn State, the Panthers were unbeaten and ranked number one in the country. It looked as if they were closing in on a national championship.

It was hard to imagine the Panthers letting down, but against cross-state rival Penn State, Pitt had its only bad game of the year. Dan threw two scoring passes on his club's first two possessions. But after that, whenever the Panthers got on a roll, something went wrong. One drive was killed by a penalty, another by a turnover. The Nittany Lions had their offense in high gear and took the lead. That meant Dan had to play catch-up football, not easy for any quarterback.

It just never came together. The final score was 48–14, the Nittany Lions on top. Dan had completed 22 of 45 passes for 267 yards and two touchdowns. Not bad numbers. But four of his passes were picked off by the Penn State defense. It was perhaps the toughest loss of Dan Marino's football life.

"When you lose a big game like that it's nice to have a family so close," Dan said. "It was reassuring to come home and talk to my dad and my family, and know they still love me."

Now all that remained was a postseason meeting in the Sugar Bowl with the highly ranked Georgia Bulldogs and their star running back, Herschel Walker.

The New Year's Day game was exciting from start to finish. Pitt seemed to dominate, but twice the Bull-dogs took the lead. In the fourth quarter, penalties hurt Pitt, and Georgia scored to take a 20–17 advantage.

With just three minutes left Dan and his teammates got the ball back at their own 20. Displaying coolness under fire, Dan began moving the Panthers upfield. He had to play the clock as well as the Georgia defense.

What it finally came down to was this—the ball was at the Georgia 33-yard line, a fourth-down play. There were just 35 seconds remaining on the clock. As he came to the line of scrimmage, Dan knew it was his last chance. He called signals and dropped straight back scanning the field. He saw his tight end, John Brown, breaking free near the end zone and he fired. The ball was right on the mark to Brown, who gathered it in as he crossed the goal line. It was a clutch throw and it won the game for Pittsburgh, the extra point making it 24–20.

For Dan it was the victory that meant the most. "The Sugar Bowl was a great victory for us," he said. "We had to redeem ourselves from the Penn

State game. . . . With the Sugar Bowl victory, we gained respect.''

The football world gained even more respect for Dan Marino. He had completed 26 of 41 passes for 261 yards and three scores. Not surprisingly, he was voted the game's Most Valuable Player. He led his team to a third-straight 11-1 season and a number-two national ranking. He was a consensus All-American selection and finished fourth in the balloting for the Heisman Trophy, which is given to the best college player in the country.

He had completed 226 of 380 passes for 2,876 yards, 59.5 percent, and a nation's best 37 touchdowns. When he returned for his senior year, it was projected that he'd be the number-one choice of the NFL the following season. It seemed that only an injury could rewrite the Marino script.

It's still difficult to explain what happened during that 1982 season. Maybe expectations were too high. Maybe the team just wasn't strong enough. Or maybe Dan just fell victim to the what-have-you-done-for-me-lately nature of sports. The bottom line was that Dan had a good senior season but not a great one. His numbers were down from the year before, and this time the Panthers lost three games.

Pittsburgh won its first seven games of the season, but in three of those contests, Dan threw for less than 200 yards. He also had just 11 TD passes and was picked off 18 times.

Then came a 31–16 loss to Notre Dame, a game against Army in which he was just 10 of 19 for 71 yards, and a 19–10 defeat by Penn State in the regular season finale. When the Panthers were beaten by SMU in the Cotton Bowl, 7–3, there was even more talk about Marino having lost the magic. He finished his senior year with 221 completions on 378 attempts for a 58.4 percentage and 2,432 yards. He threw for 17 scores, 20 fewer than the year before, and was intercepted 23 times. It was a solid performance, but now John Elway of Stanford was being talked about as the best college quarterback in the land.

It didn't matter that Dan had thrown for 8,597 yards in four years and was the all-time Pitt leader in passing and total offense by a landslide. He finished his career ranked fifth on the all-time NCAA list in passing yardage, fourth in completions (693), and fourth in touchdown passes (79). He had appeared in four straight bowl games and his team had a record of 42-5 during his tenure. Yet suddenly there were reservations among the pros because Dan simply didn't produce a consistent season.

The entire scenario was difficult to understand. Dan still had the numbers of an outstanding quarterback. His physical attributes were obvious. The so-called "bad" season saw the Panthers finish at 9-3. Yet Dan Marino wasn't rated as highly as he had been the year before. In fact, one NFL player-personnel director said that Dan had "lost his throwing rhythm completely."

Finally it was draft day. The Baltimore Colts had the first pick in the draft that year and they promptly picked John Elway of Stanford. He wasn't the only one picked ahead of Dan. Before the first round was over, quarterbacks Jim Kelly, Todd Blackledge, Tony Eason, and Ken O'Brien were also chosen. Other teams passed up the chance to pick Dan for players at other positions.

Then it was time for Miami to pick. The Dolphins'

coach, Don Shula, was not only a great field leader but also a shrewd judge of talent.

"I'd been hoping Dan would be there, but I didn't see any logical way he could," the coach said. "I'd seen him in the postseason Hula Bowl and the Senior Bowl. All he'd done was win the MVP in both. I still had him rated right up there with Elway."

When they saw that Dan was still available, the Dolphins grabbed him. He was the sixth and last quarterback taken in the first round of the 1983 draft, the 27th pick overall. This group became known as the "Class of '83," and it was Dan Marino who would jump to the head of that class.

Dan was joining an extremely successful franchise. Don Shula became coach in 1970 and promptly led the team to a 10-4 season. The club had rarely been down since then. In 1972 the Dolphins not only won their first Super Bowl but also became the only modern NFL team to go through an entire season and playoff undefeated. A year later the team won a second Super Bowl.

In the 1980s Miami was still one of the best. In 1982 the team once again made a Super Bowl appearance. This time they were beaten by Washington, 27–17.

As good as the Dolphins were, however, they didn't have a top-flight quarterback. Veteran Bob Griese had retired in 1980 and young David Woodley took over. Woodley ran Shula's precise game plans well but was not a top thrower. He was penciled in as the starter in '83, though.

Dan looked good in the preseason, but it was Woodley who saw all the action in the first two games. Even though the Dolphins won both, the team wasn't generating much offense. Then in the third game, against the L.A. Raiders, Miami fell behind early. Coach Shula felt it was time to test his prize rookie.

Not showing any sign of nervousness, Dan took his first NFL snap and dropped straight back. He looked toward the sideline and quickly zipped the ball to wideout Mark Duper for a nine-yard gain. From there he drove his team downfield and finished the drive with a six-yard TD toss to tight end Joe Rose. On the Dolphins' next possession, Marino again drove them down for a score. Unfortunately, it wasn't enough. The Raiders won the game, 27–14, but Marino had completed 11 of his first 17 NFL passes for 90 yards and two scores.

Woodley played again the following week, and the week after that Dan again pitched in relief and looked good. The Dolphins were 3-2 at this point but were dead last in the league in passing and fifth from the bottom in scoring. Coach Shula wasted no time in naming Dan the starter against Buffalo the following week.

The game was played in the Orange Bowl, in Miami, and early on it was all Buffalo. Midway through the second period the Bills had a 14–0 lead and Marino had already thrown a pair of interceptions. An ordinary rookie would have been intimidated by the shaky start, but not Dan Marino. He marched up and down on the sideline, talking to his receivers and reassuring them that they would get back in the game.

From that point on, Marino was superb. He certainly didn't play like a rookie, especially in a position that is supposed to take three to five years to learn thoroughly. The game turned into a high-scoring donnybrook that went into overtime. Unfortunately, the Miami defense wasn't equal to the task and Buffalo won it, 38–35.

But Dan Marino had been magnificent. He completed 19 of 29 passes for 322 yards and three touchdowns. There would be no more changes at quarterback. The job belonged to Dan Marino. In a matter of weeks he showed the entire league he owned it.

Once he knew the offense was his, Dan put a quick-strike tag on it. Defenses didn't know how to stop him from hitting wide receivers such as Mark Duper, Nat Moore, Duriel Harris, and rookie Mark Clayton. Running back Tony Nathan was also an outstanding receiver.

Following the Buffalo loss, Dan quarterbacked the Dolphins to four straight victories. The fourth game was a 20–17 victory over the tough San Francisco 49ers. That game vaulted Marino to the top of the AFC quarterback rankings. His 102.7 rating was mind-boggling, especially for a rookie. He was completing 60.1 percent of his passes and showing remarkable poise.

"I'm throwing the way I've always thrown," Dan said when asked about his success. "I'm reading coverages better because it's a full-time job, an all-day thing, instead of just a few hours in the afternoon. Plus I've got Coach Shula working with me."

Dan was making those talent scouts who had downgraded his rating after his senior year look like fools. He was enjoying far more success than any of the other quarterbacks picked in the first round that year. When the season ended, the Dolphins had a 12-4 mark and the AFC East title.

Dan has been an NFL star since his rookie year. This has been a familiar sight for more than a decade, Marino looking to throw the ball downfield. His quick release and rifle arm have already set many records. *(Courtesy Miami Dolphins)*

Dan had played in 11 regular-season games, starting in nine of them. He'd completed 173 of 296 passes for 2,210 yards and 20 touchdowns. Just six of his passes were picked off, and he was sacked only 10 times. His 96.0 ranking made him the first rookie to lead his conference in passing since the 1970 merger. Only Steve Bartkowski and Joe Theismann in the NFC had slightly higher ratings.

Though the Dolphins lost to Seattle, 27–20, in the first round of the playoffs, Dan's efforts resulted in his being named Rookie of the Year, as well as becoming the first rookie quarterback ever to start in the Pro Bowl. It was quite a year, but didn't fully foreshadow what was to come in 1984.

Dan Marino came out of the gate like no pro quarterback before him. The first game of that season was against Washington, and it didn't take the Redskins long to realize they were up against a passing wizard.

Dan completed 21 of 28 passes for 311 yards in a 35–17 Miami victory. Even more impressive was the fact that all five Dolphin touchdowns came on Marino scoring aerials. None of his passes were intercepted. The Redskins simply couldn't stop him.

It continued that way week after week. Dan threw the football to his receivers, and it didn't seem to matter what kind of defense he faced. With their quarterback on a record-setting pace, the Dolphins won their first 11 games. And with each passing week, Dan amazed more and more people with his ability to run a pro offense.

Though he wasn't fast, Dan was quick and clever in the pocket. He had a very solid offensive line and as a result was rarely sacked. Even when a defender did break through, Dan could usually avoid the sack or get rid of the ball with his quick-release rifle arm.

That rifle arm was producing big passing days. Against St. Louis, Dan completed 24 of 36 for 429 yards and three scores. He threw for 422 more yards in a victory over the New York Jets, and against the always-tough L.A. Raiders, he completed 35 of 57 passes for 470 yards and four touchdowns. Ironically, the Dolphins lost that one, 45–34. When the season ended the Dolphins had won the AFC East title with a 14-2 record. Dan Marino was the talk of the football world.

Dan had finished a record-breaking season in which he completed 362 of 564 passes, for 5,084 yards. Both the number of completions and yardage totals were new NFL records. He completed 64.2 percent of his passes and had an NFL-best quarterback rating of 108.9. But perhaps his most impressive record was the 48 touchdown passes he threw. The old record had been 36, which Dan just blew away. By contrast, only 17 of his tosses were intercepted.

He had been called great in college. Now Dan was being called great in the pros. His two primary wide receivers also prospered from his sensational year. Mark Clayton caught 73 passes for 1,389 yards and 18 touchdowns, while Mark Duper grabbed 71 for 1,306 yards and eight scores. But Dan threw to everyone. The Dolphins didn't have a great running game, so much depended on his strong right arm.

Now the Dolphins wanted to reach the Super Bowl. They got a fast start in the playoffs, as Dan hit on 21 of 34 passes for 262 yards and three scores in a 31–10 victory over Seattle. Next came the AFC title game. The Dolphins would be meeting Dan's hometown team, the Pittsburgh Steelers.

The game was a vivid reminder to the Steelers that they should have drafted Dan Marino. Dan hit Clayton on a 40-yard TD toss to open the scoring. The Steelers tied it and briefly held a 14–10 second-quarter lead before Marino really went to work. He hit Duper with a 41-yard scoring aerial and led another TD drive that resulted in a 24–14 halftime lead.

The Dolphins won the game, 45–28, as Dan threw for 421 yards (21 of 32) and four touchdowns. The Dolphins were AFC champs and headed for the Super Bowl, where their opponents would be the San Francisco 49ers. That set up a confrontation between Dan and the Niners' great quarterback, Joe Montana.

San Francisco had a 15-1 record during the regular season, so this was a matchup between the two best teams in football and the two top quarterbacks. As it turned out, the difference was in the defense. Miami couldn't stop Montana and his offense, while the Niners put more pressure on Marino than he had ever seen.

Dan made the first drive look easy, though. After a Niner punt, Miami got the ball at its own 36-yard line. Marino's first Super Bowl play resulted in a 25-yard pass to running back Tony Nathan. Five plays later Uwe von Schamann booted a 37-yard field goal and the Dolphins had a 3–0 lead.

Montana came right back with a multifaceted drive of his own. Mixing running plays with passes to his backs and wideouts, Montana drove his team 78 yards in eight plays for a score. The kick made it 7–3 with 3:12 left in the first period.

As expected, the Dolphins answered quickly. Start-

ing from their own 30, they marched upfield. After a
five-yard gain by Nathan, Dan completed four
straight passes, the final one a 21-yarder to tight end
Dan Johnson that brought the ball to the San Francisco two. On the next play Marino calmly stepped
back and hit Johnson again, this time in the end zone
for the score. Von Schamann's kick made it 10–7.
Both quarterbacks looked unstoppable, and it appeared that the game was going to be wide open.

The Dolphins had the lead as the second quarter
began. But that was when San Francisco's defensive
line began to pressure Marino, forcing him to hurry
passes. At the same time the Niner defensive backs
were giving the Miami wideouts a rough time, making
it very difficult for them to get open.

With Joe Montana as brilliant as ever, the Niners
scored 21 second-quarter points to take a 28–16 lead
into the locker room at halftime. It was over right
then. Another score and field goal in the third session
made it 38–16, and that was the way it ended. The
Dolphins were beaten.

Dan set Super Bowl records of 50 passes attempted
and 29 completed, but many came at the end when
the Niners were in a prevent defense. More important, Dan couldn't get his team into the end zone the
entire second half.

"Sometimes I didn't throw the ball well," he said
afterward. "Sometimes I didn't have time and sometimes guys didn't get open. They played the best any
team has played against us defensively. We knew
what we had to do—throw the ball against a four-
man line—and we didn't."

It was a tough loss, but one statistic was very
telling. Besides brilliant passing from Montana (24

of 35 for 331 yards), the Niners had rushed the ball 40 times for 211 yards. By contrast, the Dolphins ran just 9 times for 25 yards. Any attack needs balance.

Little did Marino or the Dolphins know then, but getting back to the Super Bowl would be a long and frustrating journey. In 1985 the team again won the AFC East with a 12-4 record, as Dan threw for 4,137 yards and 30 touchdowns. It hadn't been the sensational season that '84 had been, and in the AFC championship game, the team was upset by the New England Patriots, 31-14.

A year later Dan was again brilliant. He led all AFC quarterbacks with a 92.5 rating, completing 378 of 623 passes for 4,746 yards and 44 touchdowns. Both his attempts and completions set new NFL records. Unfortunately, the team's defense had slipped, and there still wasn't a strong running game to complement Marino's passing. The result was a mediocre 8-8 season.

It remained that way for the next three years. Dan continued to prove himself as one of the greatest passers the game had ever seen. And he was proving extremely durable. Marino was in there week after week and would be for more than 100 straight games by 1990.

"I'm really proud of that streak," Dan said. "Lining up and playing every week—your teammates knowing you're going to be in there. The rest of the records just come from playing every week."

In 1988 Dan threw for 4,434 yards and was sacked just six times all year. When he threw for 521 yards in a game against the Jets in October of that year, it was then the second-highest single-game total in NFL

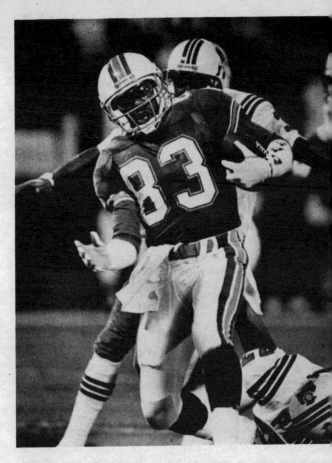

Miami wide receiver Mark Clayton has teamed with Marino to make up one of the best passing combinations in NFL history. The two have hooked up for more touchdowns than any other quaterback-receiver combo ever. *(Courtesy Miami Dolphins)*

history. A year later Dan missed his fifth 4,000-yard season by just three yards. But on September 17, 1989, he threw the 200th TD pass of his career, reaching that milestone in just 89 games, faster than any quarterback in history.

But when 1990 started, the Dolphins hadn't made the playoffs in four years, which bothered Dan more than anything.

There were even some rumblings that Dan was unhappy in Miami. These rumors were dispelled when he signed a new five-year, twenty-five-million-dollar contract that made him the highest-paid player in the NFL. The team also ran a more balanced offense. Dan didn't throw as much and went deep less frequently than he had at any time in his career. The result was a 12-4 season and a return to the playoffs.

Dan hit on 306 of 531 passes for 3,563 yards, 21 touchdowns, and just 11 intercepts. Statistically, he had had better years, but this time he had helped the team return to their winning ways.

"This was Dan's best year as far as leadership was concerned," said Coach Shula, "that and moving around in the pocket and overall toughness."

There was little doubt about how others rated Dan. Edwin Pope, a veteran sportswriter for the *Miami Herald,* ranked Dan at the top of the all-time list. And he had seen the best of them, from Sammy Baugh to John Unitas to Joe Montana.

"There is no doubt in my mind that Marino is the greatest pure passer ever to play the game," Pope said. "I've seen them all, and none of them had that God-given skill to just throw, to flick the ball like he does."

During the season Dan reached another milestone.

He had now thrown for more than 30,000 yards, reaching that mark in just 114 games, faster than anyone else in history. If he stayed healthy, many predicted he would break all the passing records before he was through.

In the team's first playoff game, against Kansas City, Dan was at his best when it counted. The tough Chiefs' defense contained him most of the afternoon, so going into the final session the Dolphins trailed, 16–3. All Marino did in that final period was complete eight straight passes (10 straight overall) for 101 yards and two touchdowns, giving the Dolphins a come-from-behind 17–16 victory.

Now it was on to the AFC title game against Buffalo. Dan played very well again, only the Miami defense wasn't up to the task, as the Bills' offense outscored the Dolphins in a 44–34 barnburner. There would be no return to the Super Bowl in 1990.

In 1991 the team once again stumbled, but Dan Marino continued to pile up the numbers on an already glorious career. Once again the Dolphins were out of the playoffs at 8-8, though Dan was outstanding the second half of the year.

After nine seasons, he was ranked second only to Joe Montana in the all-time quarterback ratings. His 266 career touchdown passes put him third on the all-time list, behind Fran Tarkenton (342) and John Unitas (290). Yet both of those QB greats had played 18 seasons. In addition, Dan had thrown more passes for more yardage than any active quarterback in the NFL. And playing a position with a high rate of injury, he had been at the helm for 124 straight games, the most consecutive QB starts since the league merger in 1970. It's amazing, more so when you consider he had five operations on his left knee, all during off-season.

It was the same old Marino in 1992. The only difference was that all of the Dolphins were also playing at his level. They got off to a fast start to jump on top of the AFC East, ahead of favored Buffalo. They finished at 11-5, the same as Buffalo. Because of a better divisional record, the Dolphins were declared AFC East champions.

Dan completed 330 of 554 passes for 4,116 yards. That made him the only NFL signal caller to go over the 4,000-yard mark in '92. He had 24 touchdowns, 16 intercepts, and a 59.6 completion percentage. His 85.1 quarterback rating was second in the AFC.

But it was the playoffs that Dan was waiting for— he wanted that elusive Super Bowl ring. The divisional game was played against the San Diego Chargers. Dan and his teammates gave the young Chargers a lesson, whipping them easily, 31–0.

Dan was 17 of 29 for 167 yards and three touchdowns. A steady rain made gripping the football difficult, but Dan took advantage of every opportunity to put points on the board. Now the Dolphins were in the AFC championship game against the defending champion Bills.

With the game played in Miami, the Dolphins were slight favorites. But the Bills came in sky-high and took the momentum from the beginning. Buffalo took a 13–3 halftime lead, which they extended to 23–3 after three quarters. Playing from behind, the Dolphins couldn't get the job done. They lost, 29–10.

Dan finished by completing 22 of 45 for 268 yards. He had been forced to throw on all but two second-half plays and was sabotaged by dropped passes all afternoon.

"It's very frustrating sitting here knowing we lost this opportunity," Dan said afterward. "Things just didn't work out. You work all year, get so close, then lose one and you're out."

Never one to make excuses, Dan will continue to throw the football with his usual excellence. He's far from finished and should continue to be great for years to come. By the time he does hang up his cleats, he'll have set passing records that will be tough to beat.

The only real question is whether he'll get another shot at the elusive Super Bowl, which is about the only world Dan Marino has yet to conquer. He's a future Hall of Famer for sure. And that's not bad for a guy who had to watch five quarterbacks picked ahead of him in 1983.

JOHN ELWAY

THERE ARE TIMES WHEN JOHN ELWAY LOOKS LIKE
Superman on a football field. Other times he appears
wild and undisciplined, like a rookie trying to find
himself. Yet no one has ever questioned the physical
credentials of the Denver Broncos' dynamic quarterback. John Elway may possess the best all-around
athletic ability and strongest throwing arm of any
quarterback in the National Football League.

When Elway came into the NFL in 1983, he was
perhaps the biggest "can't miss" quarterback prospect in years. It was a year when six highly rated
quarterbacks came out of the college ranks, and
Elway was the number-one pick of the group—the
first choice pick of the entire NFL.

That's because the 6'3", 215-pounder had just completed a career at Stanford University in which he
threw for more than 9,000 yards, ran for almost 1,000,
and tossed 77 touchdown passes, with only 39 interceptions. He also directed a pro-style offense, and

his cannon-like arm enabled him to complete passes that other quarterbacks wouldn't even attempt. Thus the "can't miss" label.

But there is nothing that guarantees a smooth transition from college to pro for anyone. There used to be an axiom that it took five years for a good college quarterback to become a good pro quarterback. But with more colleges using pro-style offenses and emphasizing the passing game, the kids coming in today are expected to adjust more quickly.

John won the starting job with the Broncos midway through his first season. Since then he has been instrumental in leading the team to three Super Bowls from 1986 to 1989. His team fell apart in each of those championship games, though, and Elway has felt the sting. What many people tend to forget is the sustained effort it takes to get to a Super Bowl. And John Elway has been putting forth that kind of effort for years.

John Albert Elway was born in Port Angeles, Washington, on June 28, 1960. His close-knit family included father Jack, mother Janet, John, and two sisters, Lee Ann and Jana. A big part of Elway family life from the beginning was football. Jack Elway was a coach. He coached high-school teams during John's early years. Then he spent four years as an assistant at Washington State University. Finally his coaching career took him and his family to California.

As a boy, however, John wasn't pushed into football. On the contrary, he was allowed to blossom into a fine, all-around athlete on his own. His father may have tutored him and given him advice, but he was never his official coach.

Young John showed great ability for throwing at

an early age. His naturally strong arm was always there, as was his enjoyment for throwing. His father was the first to notice his special talent.

"I knew he had that special kind of vision that only a few athletes have," said Jack Elway. "When he was still young and playing basketball, he could see everything on the court."

Soon after John turned 12, the Elways moved to California, where father Jack became head coach at Cal State-Northridge. In 1978 he took over at San Jose State.

When young John reached Grenada Hills High School, he really began to blossom. He was the team's starting quarterback for three years. With each season, his reputation as a star grew. Colleges began drooling over the big kid with the rifle arm. So did baseball scouts. As a power-hitting outfielder and sometimes pitcher, he had definite major-league potential.

As a senior John completed 129 of 200 passes for 1,837 yards and 19 touchdowns. He was listed on the *Parade,* Scholastic Coach, *Football News,* and National Coaches Association All-American teams. His three-year stats saw him complete 60 percent of his passes while throwing for 5,711 yards and 49 touchdowns. It was an incredible high-school career.

But football wasn't necessarily his number-one sport. As a junior he batted a sizzling .551. A year later he checked in with a .491 average, as well as a 4-2 record on the mound. He not only led Grenada Hills to the Los Angeles City championship but was also voted the Southern California CIF Baseball Player of the Year.

By that time, he was the most highly recruited

high-school athlete in the nation. Some 65 colleges were after him. Most wanted him for his quarterbacking prowess, but some wanted him for his diamond skills. He finally narrowed his choice down to two schools—Stanford University and the University of Southern California (USC).

USC had always featured a strong tailback and emphasized the running game. Stanford, on the other hand, had a tradition of producing outstanding quarterbacks and schooling them well in a pro-style passing game. Some of the quarterbacks who learned their craft with the Stanford Cardinals included John Brodie, Jim Plunkett, Guy Benjamin, Steve Dils, and Turk Schonert. All played in the NFL, as did a number of other Cardinal QBs.

This tradition, as well as Stanford's fine academic reputation, were what made John Elway decide on the Palo Alto school. Despite his stated intentions, the Kansas City Royals thought enough of his baseball talents to tab John on the 18th round of the 1979 draft. Elway wasn't ready to give up college to try his hand at professional baseball, though.

John arrived at Palo Alto with a huge reputation. The starting quarterback was slated to be Turk Schonert, who had waited for his chance while Benjamin and Dils ran the team the previous three years. They say that even Schonert looked over his shoulder at the big freshman.

"Turk felt the pressure, no question," said Jim Fassel, the Cardinals' offensive coordinator. "He knew that to play ahead of John Elway you had to be a great quarterback. It didn't matter if you were a senior and he was only a freshman."

Schonert had a brilliant year, leading the entire nation in passing. Elway played sparingly in nine games, completing 50 of 96 passes for 544 yards and six touchdowns. He had a 52.1 completion percentage and had just three passes picked off. That spring, he played with the baseball team and hit a disappointing .269, with a single home run and just 18 RBIs in 130 at-bats. Then in 1980, Elway was handed control of the Cardinal football team and the legend began.

What made John Elway's performance even more amazing was that the Cardinals were never a powerhouse team. In his final three varsity seasons, the Cardinals had a combined record of 15-18. Yet he set a host of school, conference, and NCAA passing records that impressed all the professional teams.

As a sophomore he set PAC-10 records for touchdown passes, completions, and total offense. Against Oregon State he threw for six touchdowns, four of them in a single quarter. In a game against powerful Oklahoma, he threw for three scores and ran for another as Stanford won, 31–14. After the game Oklahoma coach Barry Switzer couldn't stop praising Elway.

"John Elway put on the greatest exhibition of quarterback play and passing I've ever seen on this field," Switzer said.

When the season ended, the Cardinals were just 6-5, but John had completed 248 of 379 passes for 2,889 yards and 27 touchdowns. His completion percentage was a gaudy 65.4, and he had been picked off only 11 times. He sometimes threw the ball so hard his receivers had a difficult time catching it. He was almost unstoppable and was named to several All-American teams.

The following spring he hit .361 with the Stanford

baseball team, belting nine homers and driving in 50 runs in just 49 games. In the NCAA Central Regionals he hit .444 and was voted onto the all-tournament team. He was also outstanding in right field, his throwing arm something base runners feared.

As a junior, John was saddled with a team that lacked depth and didn't have talent. Despite his continued outstanding play, the club lost seven of its first nine games, including one to his father's San Jose State team. They wound up with a 4-7 record. Yet John Elway continued to amaze all who saw him play.

Against Purdue he completed 33 of 44 passes for 418 yards. In a game with Ohio State he hit on 21 of 27 passes in the second half, including nine in a row. He played through a succession of injuries and still couldn't be stopped. Against Arizona State he completed 10 of 17 passes for an amazing 270 yards and three touchdowns before chipping a bone in his hand and suffering a concussion.

When the long season ended he had hit 214 passes on 366 tries for 2,674 yards and 20 scores. His passing percentage was 58.4. Pro-type numbers again, and the NFL people knew it.

"Elway's got everything going for him, no negatives to speak of," said Tom Braatz, player-personnel director for the Atlanta Falcons. Everyone else seemed to agree.

That was all well and good. But the losing season hurt John, who was first and foremost a competitor.

"I've learned a lot this year," John said. "You learn more from losing, I think. Your patience gets tested and I've learned self-control."

Maybe it was the losing season that gave John the

urge for a change of pace. He signed a contract to play minor league baseball with the New York Yankees for six weeks that summer. It meant no more college baseball, but it wouldn't affect his football eligibility. The Yanks sent him to play for their Oneonta, New York, team in a Class A league, where he made $140,000.

John hit .318 for Oneonta, leading the team in RBIs, with 24. The Yanks were very high on him.

"We project him as a superstar," said Yankee vice-president Bill Bergesch, of the left-handed hitter. "He's got everything a scout looks for. He's big and strong, he can run, he can hit and hit with power. And he's got that strong arm. We see him as our right fielder down the road."

In the fall of 1982 he was back on the gridiron, and despite playing for another mediocre Stanford team that would go 5-6, John was magnificent. He had another consensus All-American season. This time he completed 262 of 405 passes for 3,242 yards and 24 touchdowns. His passing percentage was 64.7, and he was picked off just 12 times, which is amazing, since defensive teams knew he was going to throw nearly 40 times a game and he didn't have a strong running attack to complement him. Still they couldn't stop his passing.

When it was over, John had set five major NCAA Division 1-A records and nine major PAC-10 marks. He had completed 62.1 percent of his passes and thrown for 9,349 yards, with 77 touchdowns and just 39 interceptions. He finished second in the balloting for the Heisman Trophy, and made it clear that football would be his sport as a professional. If, for some reason, it didn't work out, then he always had baseball to fall back on.

Despite a slew of great quarterbacks coming out of the college ranks, there was little doubt that Elway would be the number-one choice. Jim Kelly, Dan Marino, Tony Eason, and Todd Blackledge were all highly touted, but Elway, without a doubt, was the main man.

The problem was that the team with the first pick in the 1983 draft was the Baltimore Colts. John Elway had his heart set on remaining with a West Coast team. As a potential top choice, he did the unthinkable.

"I told the Colts not to draft me," he said. "I had no intention of playing in Baltimore and I meant it. If it comes to that, I could always sign with the Yankees."

College stars aren't supposed to dictate to the pros where they will or won't play. Right away, John was labeled as a prima donna. But in truth, he was doing what more and more athletes were: trying to assume some control over his destiny. The Colts apparently thought he was bluffing. On draft day they made John Elway the first choice in the 1983 draft.

It was a draft that saw six quarterbacks go in the first round. While Tony Eason, Todd Blackledge, Ken O'Brien, and Dan Marino signed with their respective teams rather quickly, John and Jim Kelly did not.

Jim Kelly opted to start his pro career in the fledgling United States Football League. And Elway made good on his promise. He told the Colts he would not sign with them. Only a trade to a team of his liking would get him into the NFL for the 1983 season.

When John Elway drops back to pass, anything can happen. A great athlete with a great arm, Elway has engineered some incredible comebacks and miracle endings for the Denver Broncos.

(Vernon J. Biever Photo)

At first the Colts played hardball and told him that if he didn't sign with them he simply wouldn't play. But they knew that if they didn't sign him, he could reenter the draft the following year. The team wanted something out of their first pick, and on May 2 they announced a major trade.

They traded the rights to John to the Denver Broncos. In return, the Colts got the Broncos' top draft pick, along with tackle Chris Hinton, veteran quarterback Mark Herrmann, and Denver's number-one pick in 1984. In the eyes of most, the Colts had practically given John away. Denver wasn't on the West Coast, but it was close enough and appealed to John. He soon signed his first pro contract, a five-year deal worth approximately five million dollars.

Dan Reeves, the team coach, was a former Dallas running back and an assistant under the Cowboys' highly successful long-time coach, Tom Landry. Under Reeves, the Broncos were 10-6 in 1981 but failed to make the playoffs. Then in the strike-shortened 1982 season, the ballclub fell to 2-7. Denver fans felt they didn't have much hope for the immediate future. But the trade on May 2, 1983, changed everything. In John Elway, fans felt they were getting that rare commodity: a franchise quarterback, a guy who would lead the team for the next dozen years.

Veteran Steve DeBerg was penciled in as the starting quarterback in 1983, but many felt Elway would take over before the year ended. The Broncos' offense was considered spotty. There was no star running back, only one All-Pro quality receiver in Steve Watson, and an average offensive line. It was the defense, led by linebackers Randy Gradishar and

Tom Jackson and cornerback Louis Wright, that was considered the heart of the team.

The publicity generated by Elway's signing was enormous. John knew he would be under tremendous pressure to produce, but he didn't want people to think he was somehow special.

"I'm an ordinary guy," he told the press, "a low-key guy. But I'm not perfect and I like to horse around. Guess I'm still a little kid at heart."

A little kid, maybe, but one with a major-league throwing arm. The team would be playing the Seattle Seahawks in its first preseason game. Veteran De-Berg played the first half, but everyone in the stands wanted the rookie. At the beginning of the second half, they got him.

The Broncos had the ball at their own 35-yard line. After a running play was brought back by a penalty, John dropped back to pass. His first NFL throw was a six-yard completion to running back Rick Parros. Next he hit running back Dave Preston for six. Then came a nine-yard throw to wideout Rick Upchurch. First down.

After an incomplete pass, Elway lined up in the shotgun for the first time. He looked downfield, took the snap, kept his poise in the pocket, and rifled a 38-yard strike to wide receiver Steve Watson. The crowd went wild. The savior had arrived. Two plays later he fired the ball between two defenders to Up-church for a 16-yard gain to the two. Running back Sammy Winder then punched it over for the touch-down. Again, the crowd roared. John Elway's first appearance had resulted in a 65-yard touchdown drive.

John's great potential shone throughout the preseason. Finally Coach Reeves decided there was no reason to hold the rookie back. He named John Elway his starting quarterback for the regular season.

John's rookie season was a learning one. He found out about the brutal banging a pro quarterback can take. He hurt his elbow in the opener at Pittsburgh after completing just one of his first eight passes. De-Berg finished up and the Broncos won. A week later a slight shoulder injury sent him to the sidelines after he'd completed 9 of 21 tosses for just 106 yards.

Against Philadelphia he completed 18 of 33 for 193 yards and his first pro TD pass. But he also had two throws picked off, and the Broncos lost. A concussion the following week limited him to part-time play for that game and the next one. But when DeBerg was hurt against Seattle, John was back in action.

His two best games in 1983 were in the 14th and 15th weeks. He completed 16 of 24 passes for 284 yards and two scores in a 27–6 victory over Cleveland and then threw for three touchdowns and 345 yards in a 21–19 win over Baltimore. In that one, John completed 23 of 44 passes and didn't have an interception.

The Broncos finished the year with a 9-7 record and were in the playoffs. They lost to Seattle, 31–7, in the wild-card playoff game.

John didn't have big numbers that first year. He completed just 123 of 259 passes for 1,663 yards and a mediocre 47.5 completion percentage. In addition, he threw just 7 touchdown passes as opposed to 14 interceptions and was the 17th-ranked passer in the AFC. The pressure on John, however, had been enormous. He admitted he had "a lot to learn" but looked forward to 1984. All the Broncos did.

Yes, 1984 was a turnaround. John had the support of a 1,000-yard rusher in Sammy Winder and a 1,000-yard receiver in Steve Watson, and had an outstanding season. Coupled with the swarming Denver defense, the Broncos won the AFC West title with a franchise-best 13-3 record. In the 14 games John started, the Broncos were 12-2.

For the year he completed 214 of 380 passes for 2,598 yards and 18 touchdowns. His completion percentage was 56.3, and he had just 15 picked off. He was also third on the team in rushing, with 237 yards on 56 carries. He began exhibiting the ability that would become his trademark in the NFL—bringing his team from behind in the fourth quarter, often with spectacular clutch passing. In 1984 he did it three times.

The entire club was optimistic entering the playoffs. But they were beaten by Pittsburgh, 24–17. It was a disappointment, yet the club was getting closer. That's why 1985 left everyone hanging. The Broncos were a solid 11-5 for the year but didn't make the playoffs. Usually a team with that kind of mark makes it as a wild card—not that time.

But for John Elway, it was his best year yet. He led the NFL with 605 passing attempts, completing 327 for 3,891 yards and 22 scores. Add his 253 yards rushing and his total offense was over 4,000 yards, the best in the entire league. He also brought his team from behind four times with fourth-quarter clutch drives. He was becoming known as the league's most spectacular quarterback in the closing minutes of a close game.

The Denver defense also continued to shine, with Rulon Jones, Karl Macklenburg, Dennis Smith, and

Louis Wright all making the Pro Bowl. So once again optimism was the byword when 1986 rolled around.

John had a consistent and steady season, and the well-balanced Broncos won their first six games, then cruised to the AFC West title with an 11-5 record. John threw for nearly 3,500 yards, completed 55.6 percent of his passes, and connected with 19 receivers in the end zone. It was his first Pro Bowl season, and he received a number of other postseason honors, including being presented with the Seattle Gold Helmet Award as Professional Football Player of the Year.

Only the playoffs mattered now. In the first round the Broncos would be meeting the New England Patriots. It was a see saw contest all the way. John wasn't having one of his better games, and many of his passes were off the mark.

It was a 10–10 game at halftime. Denver drew first blood in the third quarter on a Rich Karlis field goal. But then New England's Tony Eason hit Stanley Morgan with a 45-yard touchdown strike, and the Pats forged ahead to a 17–13 advantage. John knew it was time to get down to business. Denver started on its own 14 and began driving. Five plays later they were on the New England 48.

John dropped back to pass. He sidestepped one defender and threw the ball deep. Vance Johnson took it home for a 48-yard touchdown. With the game on the line, John Elway had come through again. Karlis's point after made it 20–17. The only scoring in the final session was a safety, when Eason was tackled by Rulon Jones in the end zone. The two points made it a 22–17 final. The Broncos were in the AFC championship game against Cleveland—one step away from the Super Bowl.

The first half was almost identical to the New England game. By halftime the game was deadlocked at 10–10. A Rich Karlis field goal gave the Broncos a 13–10 lead after three periods. But in the fourth quarter a Mark Moseley field goal followed by a 48-yard TD toss from quarterback Bernie Kosar gave the Browns a 20–13 lead. Now time was running down. There was just 5:43 left in the game as the Browns kicked off.

It was a low kickoff that was bobbled, and as John trotted onto the field his team was 98 yards from the Cleveland goal line. There was just 5:32 left on the clock.

"If you work hard, good things are going to happen," John told his teammates in the huddle. Then he smiled and went to work. First he hit Sammy Winder with a short pass for several yards. Next he scrambled 11 yards for a first down. On the next play he dropped back and connected with Steve Sewell for a 22-yard gain and another first. Steve Watson caught the next pass for a 12-yard gain and the Broncos had a first down at the Cleveland 40. There was now just 1:59 left.

Then suddenly there was trouble. After an incomplete pass, the Browns' defense sacked Elway for an 8-yard loss, back to the 48. Working from the shotgun, John completed a clutch 20-yard pass to Mark Jackson at the 28. First down. After another incompletion, the redoubtable Elway hit Sewell for a 14-yard gain to the 14. First down again. There were now just 57 seconds left.

John scrambled out of the pocket and ran nine

yards to the Cleveland five. On third and one he dropped back and threw a bullet to Mark Jackson in the end zone for the score. The impossible had happened. John Elway had taken his team 98 yards in the closing minutes. Then Rich Karlis tied the game with the extra point. Elway's heroics were forever stamped simply as The Drive.

The game, however, was still up for grabs. In overtime, John drove his team to the Cleveland 15 and then let Rich Karlis kick the 33-yard field goal that won it. The Broncos were in the Super Bowl, and John's reputation as a fourth-quarter, game-on-the-line gunslinger grew even more.

In Super Bowl XXI, played at the Rose Bowl in Pasadena, California, the Broncos would be meeting the tough New York Giants. The Giants were a ball-control team with a great defense led by all-world linebacker Lawrence Taylor. They were 9- or 10-point favorites.

"We knew we'd be the underdog," John said. "But . . . it'll be a zero–zero game when it starts."

Denver took the opening kickoff and John drove them 45 yards to the Giants' 31. Rich Karlis then booted a 48-yard field goal to give the Broncos a 3–0 lead. The Giants then drove 78 yards for a touchdown. Phil Simms, the veteran quarterback, hit six straight passes, including a six-yarder to tight end Mark Bavaro for the score. The kick made it a 7–3 game.

On the next series the Broncos were starting from their own 42 and drove 58 yards for another score. Karlis's kick made it a 10–7 game. Then came a turning point. In the second quarter the Broncos drove again. John completed a 54-yard bomb to Vance Johnson on the Giants' 28. Seven plays later, the Broncos had a first and goal at the Giants' one-yard line.

But the New York defense held on three straight plays. Then Karlis missed a 23-yard field-goal try. Denver had come up empty. The only other scoring in the second quarter came when John was tackled in his own end zone for a safety. So Denver had a slim 10–9 lead at halftime.

Then in the third quarter the roof fell in. The Giants scored 20 unanswered points, and that made it a 29–10 game. The final score was 39–20. The Giants were Super Bowl champs.

Simms had put on a great show, completing 22 of 25 passes for 268 yards, while Elway, who also had a fine day, connected on 22 of 37 for 304 yards. But the bottom line was that the Broncos were beaten badly. Now the team felt it had something to prove.

The 1987 season saw a three-game players' strike, and because of the strike it was only a 15-game season. Denver finished at 10-4-1 to win the AFC West once again.

John Elway had been sensational. In the 12 games he played, he completed 224 of 410 passes for 3,198 yards and a 54.6 percentage. He threw for 19 touchdowns with just 12 interceptions and was named the NFL's Most Valuable Player by the Associated Press. John seemed to have finally silenced the critics who claimed he had never reached his vast potential.

In the playoffs John started off brilliantly. He completed 14 of 25 passes for 259 yards as the Broncos ripped the Houston Oilers, 34–10. Then came a return match with Cleveland. Memories of "The Drive" returned, and this game was even wilder. Both offenses shone.

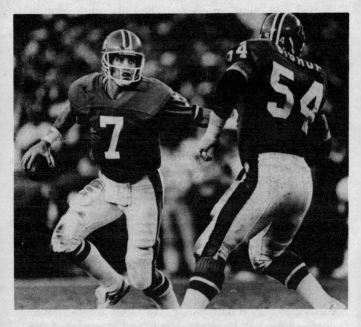

This is a sight Broncos opponents have learned to fear. Elway is on the move, looking downfield for a receiver. More often than not, he'll find one and rifle the ball home whether on the run or in the pocket. *(Vernon J. Biever Photo)*

Cleveland's Bernie Kosar was just as brilliant as Elway, though John was the more spectacular. At one point he completed an 80-yard scoring strike to Mark Jackson. Denver led 21–3 at the half. But a big third quarter cut the Bronco lead to 31–24. When Cleveland scored again in the fourth, the game was tied at 31–31. Denver then took the kickoff to its own 25, and when Elway came onto the field there was just 5:14 left in the game. Shades of 1986.

Once again John drove his team with the game on the line. He fired a 26-yard pass to Rickey Nattiel. Then three plays later he hit Nattiel for 26 more, bringing the ball to the Cleveland 20. On the next play, John hit running back Sammy Winder, who took it all the way to the end zone for the go-ahead score. In the closing minutes, Denver took an intentional safety to use up the clock and won the game, 38–33. They were in the Super Bowl once more.

In the Super Bowl, the Broncos met the Washington Redskins at Jack Murphy Stadium in San Diego. Washington went nowhere on its first series. Denver got the ball in good field position at its own 44.

Elway crouched over center. He checked the defense and called signals. Then he dropped back to pass, looking deep. He spotted rookie wideout Rickey Nattiel and flicked his powerful arm. The ball sailed in a high arc toward the Washington goal. When it came down, Nattiel grabbed the pass and ran it into the end zone. Elway and the Broncos had struck on their first offensive play of the game, a 56-yard TD toss.

By the end of the first period the Broncos had a 10–0 lead and appeared to be well in control. What happened in the next 15 minutes is still difficult to believe. With veteran quarterback Doug Williams at the controls, the Redskins scored 35 unanswered points, all in the second period. As a team, the Redskins racked up 356 yards of total offense in 15 minutes. The Broncos were shellshocked and beaten.

"It all snowballed on us," John said. "By not getting some points [in the second period] and slowing them down it hurt us. That was the most disappointing thing. We never answered the bell in that second quarter."

The final score was 42–10, and the Broncos were soundly defeated for a second straight time.

Then the team slumped to 8-8 in 1988. Though John threw for 3,309 yards and completed 55.2 percent of his passes, it was looked upon as a poor year. He threw for 17 touchdowns but was intercepted 19 times and he finished 18th in the quarterback ratings. It was said he was inconsistent and didn't have the pinpoint accuracy of a Joe Montana or the controlled precision of a Dan Marino.

In 1989 the Broncos started well. The team won six of its first seven games. Yet in Denver, it had become fashionable to criticize John Elway.

John said that people watched everything he did. "They talk about my teeth, they talk about my hair, how much I tip, how I'm playing and when I'll talk to the media. I'm sick of it," he said. "I don't want to sound like a crybaby, but it's just gotten to be too much lately. It's tearing me up inside."

Because of John's great physical ability, people expected big numbers. But it wasn't always within the scheme of the Denver offense for the quarterback to produce the numbers. Landing his team in two straight Super Bowls apparently wasn't enough. John

Elway was expected to win. He said the offense had changed slightly during the first half of '89.

"We've been playing more of a ball-control game this year," he said, explaining why he had racked up only modest passing numbers. "But I think we've got to start looking for the big play more than we have."

The one real rap on John was that he had never become a "touch" passer. He rarely floated a pass to a certain spot. He would rather use his great arm to fire the ball through the smallest opening in the defense. While his numbers in 1989 weren't that great, he was still the most dangerous quarterback in the fourth quarter.

One writer put it this way: "Don't let mistakes kill you in the first half, and if you're behind in the second half, turn the greatest street-ball quarterback in history loose. . . . For one of the worst-rated passers in the league this season, he sure turns up on a lot of highlight shows, doesn't he?"

For sure. The team finished with an 11-5 record to regain the AFC West crown. As for John, he threw for 3,051 yards, completing 53.6 percent of his passes. His 18 touchdown passes were offset somewhat by 18 interceptions. It might have been an off year statistically, but he won. That was the bottom line.

Once again the Broncos marched toward the Super Bowl. First the team squeaked by Pittsburgh, 24–23, then had another AFC title game meeting with Cleveland. This time John didn't need a fourth-quarter drive. He threw for 385 yards and three scores. The Broncos won, 37–21. Now the team was headed to the Super Bowl for the third time in four years.

Waiting for the Broncos was the team considered the best in football, the San Francisco 49ers. The

Niners would be trying to win their fourth Super Bowl of the decade. They were quarterbacked by the impeccable Joe Montana. John knew that he would ultimately be measured by his Super Bowl successes or failures. Montana had already won three and was being called by some the best of all time.

"I just want to go to bat again," John said. "We'll give it all we got. If we lose, we lose, and if we win, we're world champs." John knew he was the main man come crunch time.

"When it's third and six . . . they're still looking to me to pick up that first down. But I think this is the best team I've ever been on going to a Super Bowl, but we may be playing the best team that's ever played in the Super Bowl. That makes it tougher."

Because the Broncos had been blown out of two straight Super Bowls, no one really expected it to happen again. But John and his teammates never had a chance. Montana and the Niners played an almost perfect game. They scored two touchdowns in each of the four quarters and won in a walk, 55–10. While Montana completed 22 of 29 passes for 297 yards and 5 touchdowns, John hit on only 10 of 26 for 108 yards. But he was playing from behind right from the start, and everyone knew he had to throw. Yet John wouldn't make excuses.

"The 49ers combined good coverages with good pressure and I couldn't throw the ball to [my receivers] or get it completed," he said. "I'm definitely disappointed by the way I played. But all I can do is try to do the best I can. Sometimes that's enough and sometimes it isn't. It wasn't enough today, that's for sure."

But football is a team game. It always has been. Quarterbacks sometimes get too much of the credit and, conversely, have to take too much of the blame. Ironically, one of those who defended Elway was Joe Montana, the winning quarterback.

"Elway doesn't have to prove himself to anybody," said Super Joe. "He's proven himself over and over again."

That was certainly true. He proved it in high school, then many times at Stanford, and many times in the pros. How can anyone forget "The Drive" in the 1986 playoffs, or any of his other impossible comebacks when no one could catch him scrambling out of the backfield or defend against his clutch throws?

Whether John Elway will ever get his Super Bowl redemption remains uncertain. It didn't help when the Broncos crashed to a 5-11 season in 1990. Ironically, John had a career-best of 58.6 completion percentage that year, throwing for 3,526 yards with 15 TDs and 14 interceptions. But losing doesn't help anyone.

In 1991 Coach Reeves agreed to let John call most of his own plays. With John producing a fine season and some team balance restored, the Broncos ended with a surprising 12-4 campaign. Once again they were AFC West champs.

Against Houston in the divisional playoff, John rallied the Broncos from a 21–6 deficit. He was his old self, completing clutch passes and not wavering. He threw for 257 yards as Denver won, 26–24. Once again the Broncos were one step away from the Super Bowl.

Only this time they didn't make it. The powerful Buffalo Bills defeated them as John had to leave the game in the fourth quarter with a thigh injury. So he wouldn't have a chance to try once again for that elusive final victory.

Then came 1992 and another letdown. The Broncos again seemed headed for a playoff berth when John went on the injured-reserve list with a bad shoulder. In his absence the team faltered, and while he returned for the final game, the team finished at 8-8. He did reach one important milestone: passing the 30,000-yard mark for his career, a record reached by only a handful of quarterbacks.

When the season ended, John received another honor, one that had nothing to do with his great passing arm. He was named the 1992 Man of the Year by the National Football League, a tribute for the more than one million dollars he raised for child-abuse programs.

"It's such an atrocity to me to see that people treat children like that," John said upon accepting the award. Children have always been very special to him. He and his wife, Janet, have four.

John had surgery to fix his left shoulder in the off-season. He also learned that long-time Bronco coach Dan Reeves would be replaced for 1993. John will be 33 years old at the outset of the '93 season. Whether he will get another chance to win the big one is a question mark. Either way, he has brought something special to the game.

His talents are not the same as those of a Montana or a Marino. Some have called him a throwback to a simpler and happier time in the NFL, when quarterbacks called their own plays and often had to improvise to win. Maybe John Elway would have been appreciated more in the 1950s or 1960s. But playing today hasn't been so bad either.

Fourth quarter. Your team losing by a few points. Time running down. A chance for one more drive to win it. Who would you want at the helm, directing the offense, getting ready to pass when the defense knows a pass is coming? The answer is simple: John Elway. He's the guy who can pull a rabbit out of the hat, especially when the game is on the line.

JIM KELLY

TOUGH, TALENTED, AND A LEADER. YOU CAN'T ASK for more, especially if you're a professional quarterback. Mention these three words to fans of the Buffalo Bills, and they'll probably tell you they were invented to describe their quarterback, Jim Kelly. Since his arrival in Buffalo in 1986, Kelly has grown along with the team and helped take the Bills to three straight Super Bowls.

That isn't the entire Jim Kelly story, though. The fans wanted him in Buffalo three years earlier, when he was the team's number-one draft choice from the fabled Class of '83 college draft. Jim Kelly, for his own reasons, decided to cast his lot with the fledgling United States Football League and became a USFL record-setter for two years. When the USFL shut down, Jim signed with Buffalo and made the Bills' wait worthwhile.

Six foot three and nearly 220 pounds, Jim would seem to be the prototype of the modern quarterback.

His size and strength are exceptional. In fact, Penn State coach Joe Paterno recruited him heavily—as a linebacker. Jim would have none of it. He went to the University of Miami to be a quarterback. It was Kelly who started the long line of pro-style signal callers at Miami. He was followed to the Sunshine State by Bernie Kosar, Vinnie Testaverde, Steve Walsh, Craig Erickson, and the 1992 Heisman Trophy winner, Gino Torretta.

In the minds of many Kelly is still the best, though he'd get strong competition from the Browns' Bernie Kosar. Jim, however, didn't come out of college with an All-American or Heisman Trophy season behind him. He spent nearly his entire senior year rehabilitating a severe injury to his right shoulder, an injury that required surgery. So when Jim was being drafted by Buffalo and coveted by the USFL, there was still doubt that his throwing arm would be one hundred percent.

James Edward Kelly was born on February 14, 1960, in Pittsburgh, Pennsylvania, the same hometown as Dan Marino. Jim was the fourth son born to Joe and Alice Kelly. Twin boys followed, so there were six young Kelly boys to raise.

The family settled in East Brady, Pennsylvania, a small town located some 70 miles northeast of Pittsburgh. Mr. Kelly was a machinist at Daman Industries and had to work hard to support his wife and six growing boys. And grow they did. All six wound up over six feet and more than 210 pounds. As youngsters the six really caused havoc at home. "We'd put our helmets on and play football right in the house," Jim recalled. "We drove my mom nuts. Then we'd go to relatives' houses and break all our cousins' toys.

No matter where he's played, Jim Kelly has always shown the same toughness and tenacity. One look at the expression on his face shows the concentration that has made Jim a winner.

(Vernon J. Biever Photo)

Sometimes we'd sneak a basketball rim into our living room, put it on the wall, and play."

So the Kelly household was pretty wild. But Mr. Kelly didn't mind. He was raised in an orphanage and for that reason was always happy to have his large family around him. He also had a soft spot for sports and felt he had missed something because he had never had the time to play. So he always encouraged the boys, sometimes downright pushed them, especially young Jim.

"Jim had something a little bit extra," Mr. Kelly once said. "A little more than the other boys. I felt that all he needed was a little push to become great."

At age ten Jim became a national semifinalist in his age group in the Punt, Pass, and Kick contest. From then on, his father really encouraged him to pursue the game. If Mr. Kelly was working the afternoon or night shift and Jim came home from school for lunch, the two would practice football before eating.

"He pushed me so hard it was unbelievable," Jim said. "He wouldn't let me eat until I'd worked out. Sometimes there wouldn't be time to eat and it reached a point where sometimes I wouldn't come home because I just didn't want to practice."

There are those who would probably say that pushing a youngster that hard is wrong. Mr. Kelly's tactics could have backfired and Jim could have grown to hate football. Fortunately, that didn't happen. Jim is happy today that his father insisted on working with him.

"I'm really glad now that my father was that way," he said. "I think I'd do the same thing for my son."

By the time Jim reached East Brady High he was a full-fledged star in both football and basketball. He became a starter in basketball early and by his senior year was the star of the team.

On the gridiron he was even better. He was the quarterback on offense, and a safety and linebacker on defense. He won the starting signal-calling job as a sophomore, and until he graduated the team was undefeated. During his high-school career, he threw for 3,915 yards with 44 touchdown passes.

"We were usually so far ahead of everyone by half-time that Jim sometimes sat out most of the second half," his coach, Terry Henry, said of Jim's senior year. "Sometimes it seemed that his only incompletions were drops. I remember one game when he was 14 of 16 with two passes that just bounced off his receivers' hands.

"His senior year he was the all-conference punter, place kicker, safety, quarterback, and league player of the year. I still think he's good enough to be an NFL punter if he had to."

It goes without saying that Jim was heavily recruited. He was most interested in Penn State, but Joe Paterno began recruiting Jim as a linebacker. Jim was an outstanding quarterback, and that was the position he wanted to continue playing.

So Jim looked south and picked Miami, which might seem an odd choice for a tough kid from rural Pennsylvania. But in the fall of 1978 he headed for the Sunshine State. He was redshirted that season, then joined the varsity in 1979. He would play in seven games that year, starting four of them. His first start that year was against Penn State. To make matters worse, the game was played on the Nittany Lions' home field, putting Jim and the Hurricanes on enemy turf.

On Miami's first offensive play, Jim was hit by defensive tackle Bruce Clark, and the blow partly dislocated his jaw. His teammates expected to see another quarterback in the game, but after a few minutes with the trainer, Jim was running back onto the field.

After the injury, Jim simply dominated the game. He played with confidence and poise riddling the Penn State defense with precision passes. When the smoke cleared, Miami had a 26–10 upset victory and the Jim Kelly story had begun.

Jim wound up completing 48 of 104 passes in his first varsity season. That was only a 46.2 completion percentage—not real good. But the team was getting better. A year later he became the starter and grew even more. He completed 109 of 206 passes for 1,519 yards, 11 touchdowns, and just seven interceptions. His completion percentage was up to 52.9. They weren't huge numbers, but Jim helped the Hurricanes break into the top 20.

However, he didn't make any All-American teams and still wasn't acknowledged as one of the premier signal callers in the college ranks. That began changing in 1981, changing rapidly.

Miami began to win, and now the Hurricanes were among the top 10 teams in the country. Jim started all 11 games in their 9-2 season. Among the wins was another upset over Penn State, 17–14, a victory that might have cost the Nittany Lions the national championship. Penn State's Joe Paterno must have *wished* Jim Kelly had become a linebacker.

When the season ended, the Associated Press had the Hurricanes ranked eighth in the country. And Jim Kelly was beginning to attract attention. He completed 168 of 285 passes for 2,403 yards and 14 touchdowns. He was intercepted the same number of times, and had his completion percentage up to 59.0. Yet he still didn't make any major All-American teams and wasn't even considered as a Heisman Trophy candidate.

It was before his senior year in 1982 that Jim finally began getting some recognition. In fact, more and more preseason polls and analyses were mentioning him in the same breath with Elway, Marino, Blackledge, and Eason.

Jim looked sharp in his first two games, both victories. In the third game, against Virginia Tech, Jim was sailing along once more. Then in the third quarter, he took off on a 20-yard scramble before being hit hard by several Tech tacklers. He got up holding his right shoulder and walked slowly to the sideline. No one knew it just then, but Jim Kelly had just played his last game as a collegian.

His shoulder injury was serious. Worse yet, it was to his throwing shoulder. He needed surgery. At the time of his injury, Jim was on his way to an outstanding, All-American season. He had completed 51 of 81 passes for 585 yards and three scores. His completion percentage was a career-best 63.0. But suddenly Jim Kelly had to worry if he would still have a career.

Now, while the Elways, Marinos, Easons, and Blackledges did their thing on the field, Jim Kelly concerned himself with rigorous rehabilitation. He remembers one incident some two months after the surgery. He drove with some friends up to Tallahassee to watch the Florida–Florida State game. Jim was riding in the back of a pickup when some kids in a Volkswagen drove by.

"We were wearing Miami hats and the people in

the VW shouted a wisecrack about Miami guys," Jim remembered. "For some reason I had a lemon in my hand, and I just wound up and chucked it at the car."

It was a move that could have ended Jim's football career. "The pain, oh my God," said Jim, recalling what happened. "I fell down and lay there in the bed of the truck for about ten minutes. All I could think was 'How stupid can a human be?' "

After that, Jim was much more careful. He wanted his shoulder ready for the next season, his first as a pro.

In 1983, a new league was forming, the United States Football League. The USFL would be playing a spring schedule, so it wouldn't compete directly with the NFL. Players drafted by the USFL in 1983 wouldn't begin playing until the spring of 1984. That would give Jim's shoulder more time to heal. But that wasn't what Jim was thinking as he awaited the draft.

Jim became the first-round pick of the NFL Buffalo Bills, the third quarterback taken on the first round. With the USFL, however, he was only a 12th-round pick, taken by the Chicago Blitz. There didn't seem much doubt about where he'd go.

But Jim's agent, Greg Lustig, felt there was a good case for him to negotiate with the new league.

"I told everybody in the USFL that they could sign all the running backs in the world," said Lustig. "Guys like Herschel Walker, Tim Spencer, and Kelvin Bryant, top players and big names. But quarterbacks are the guys. Quarterbacks bring credibility."

By May of 1983 it looked like the Bills. Buffalo had offered Jim $2.1 million for four years, but only partly guaranteed. Then Lustig got a call from Bruce Allen, general manager of the Blitz.

"Hold everything," Allen said. "The USFL will make you an offer you can't refuse."

"We were this close to signing with the Bills," said Lustig. "I mean, the next word out of my mouth was going to be 'yes.' "

By that time the other first-round quarterback choices from the Class of '83—Elway, Blackledge, Eason, Ken O'Brien, and Marino—had already committed to the NFL. The USFL needed Kelly, and they were ready to give him everything he wanted, including his choice of teams.

So Jim and Lustig began negotiating with the Houston Gamblers. They finally agreed on an innovative contract with all kinds of escalating clauses. It was basically a five-year, four-million-dollar deal, but if other quarterbacks came into the league at higher salaries, Jim's would increase as well.

"I got every dime I could from the Gamblers," said Lustig, "but I don't think I stole from them. They don't feel that way, either. There was never a voice raised. I was asking for something sophisticated and they understood it."

As for Jim, he was overjoyed at the work his agent had done. "What can you say about a guy who gets you the best contract in the history of pro football?" he said.

Once he signed, Jim immediately began doing things for every member of his family. He had his parents' house remodeled and refurnished, and he sent all his brothers on a cruise to Acapulco. He then set one of his brothers up in business, paid the college tuition of another, and helped the others every way he could.

"All I'm doing is what anybody in my family would do if they were in my position," Jim said.

Now he had to produce. When he finally went to training camp in the spring, his shoulder was in good shape, although still slightly numb from the nerve damage. He had to loosen up for much longer than other quarterbacks. But once he did, he was capable of throwing the football some 70 yards.

Most experts didn't give the USFL much of a chance to survive. The league did have some outstanding running backs, like Herschel Walker and Kelvin Bryant, as well as some outstanding players at other positions. But Jim Kelly was the only so-called glamour quarterback they had signed. So there was pressure on Jim from day one.

Once at Houston, Jim met the Gamblers' offensive coordinator, "Mouse" Davis. Davis had devised an innovator, fast-strike offense called the run-and-shoot. And in Jim Kelly, he felt he had the perfect man to pull the trigger.

With the run-and-shoot, the quarterback rarely drops back into the protection of the traditional passing pocket. Instead, he sprints out, reads the defense, and then throws on the move to one of a group of quick, mobile receivers, hopefully hitting him before the secondary can adjust. There is no tight end and only one running back.

Jim's first year with Houston was like one big highlight film. Among other things he threw at least one touchdown pass in every regular-season game. At one point he had five straight games of 300 yards or more passing. Against the Jacksonville Bulls he completed 20 of 23 passes for 362 yards.

When the 1984 season ended, Jim Kelly had thrown

for 5,219 yards and added 44 touchdown passes. Both figures were records for professional football at the time. Jim was named the league's Most Valuable Player. He had been worth every cent the Gamblers paid to get him. The problem was that many people didn't consider the USFL a professional league.

A year later he was at it again. Despite missing four games with a knee injury, Jim was incredible. In his first game, against the Los Angeles Express, he completed 35 of 54 passes for 574 yards and five touchdowns! Later in the year he had a four-game stretch in which he averaged 418 yards and four touchdowns a game. He also had a streak of 120 passes without an interception. Team owner Dr. Jerry Argovitz simply called him "The Franchise."

The 1985 season saw Jim throw for 4,623 yards and 39 touchdowns. In two USFL seasons he completed 713 of 1,154 passes for 9,842 yards, 83 touchdowns, and just 45 interceptions. His completion percentage of 63.3 was also outstanding. In addition, he ran the ball 113 times for 663 yards and six more touchdowns. In 32 games he was over 300 yards passing 16 times and over 400 yards on three occasions. The Gamblers were a combined 22-10 in games he started. The only negative was that he had to endure 110 sacks. Such is the run-and-shoot.

Just about that time, however, the USFL began having major financial problems. The league had to reorganize. They tried to switch to a fall schedule and combine several franchises. It didn't work. They went out of business prior to the 1986 NFL season.

Buffalo still held the NFL rights to Jim, and the Bills were a sorry lot. The team was just 2-14 in 1984 and again in '85. No wonder Jim wasn't very enthusiastic about playing for them.

Jim had the option of sitting out the 1986 season to become a free agent the following year, free to sign with any team.

Center Kent Hull, who had played against Jim with the New Jersey Generals, met Jim at the Generals' minicamp in 1986. He saw how much playing football meant to the quarterback.

"Before I met him I figured he'd sit the year out and hold an auction," said Hull. "But after I met him I knew there was no way he could be out of football for a year."

Hull, who also signed with the Bills, was right. On August 18 it was announced that Jim Kelly had come to terms with the Buffalo Bills, signing a multiyear deal worth some eight million dollars. Jim was going to a team that had won just four games in two years. He would be a player around whom the Bills could build. As Bills' coach Hank Bullough said, "Jim Kelly is our future."

The impact Jim made on the city of Buffalo as well as the Bills even before he played a single game was staggering. The Bills were an original American Football League team, formed with the new league in 1960. They became the class of the AFL with a pair of championships in the mid-1960s. After the two leagues merged, the Bills had a couple of solid seasons in the mid-1970s, when O. J. Simpson became a record-breaking running back. There was a divisional title in 1980 and a wild-card playoff berth the next year. Then hard times returned.

Now Jim Kelly was coming. Ticket sales soared.

The blue-collar workers in Buffalo loved him from the first.

"He's a good guy and he's a tough guy," said Coach Bullough. "When he signed the contract, people said, 'Boy, he got a lot of money.' I said, 'No, he didn't. He got the market value.' If he had waited a year and then let people bid for him he could have gotten a lot more. Ninety percent of the players in his position would have waited. But Jim's a football player. He wants to play."

Because he signed late, Jim had time for only 19 full practices before the season opener, against the New York Jets. He had to learn a whole new system, and it wasn't easy.

"Sometimes your head starts hurting," Jim said. "You feel that you just can't absorb any more football. The whole point is that I don't want to embarrass myself out there—or my teammates. For instance, I still have to think about the language, the terminology. Getting into a new set of terms is a problem. It's like being in a foreign country and trying to speak the language."

The Jets were ready to give Kelly a dose of NFL football. "Jim Kelly will get a pass rush tomorrow, he can count on that," said Jets' defensive coordinator Bud Carson. "Our guys are anxious to indoctrinate him. This is not the U.S. Football League. I'm sure that someday he's going to be a great quarterback, but when they knock you down in this league, you don't get up right away."

If that statement was meant to intimidate Jim, it didn't work. Jim wasn't intimidated by anyone. When game time arrived, he knew he had to be ready. He had only played in a single preseason contest, so he was starting from scratch.

But Jim came out and led the Buffalo offense like a seasoned veteran. Despite the Jets' pass rush, Jim held the ball to the last possible second before releasing it. The Jet defenders saw early on that he was willing to take major hits to get his passes off.

Near the end of the first half he was knocked dizzy by the Jets' defense. Later, New York's Mark Gastineau blindsided him and bruised his back. He also twisted an ankle, but he hung in there and refused to budge. In the fourth period he brought his club back to take a three-point lead, 17–14. But the Jets surged against the Buffalo defense and scored twice to go ahead, 28–17.

Once again Jim drove his team. With the ball at the Jets' four, Jim took the snap and fell as he began to pull away from center. Some QBs would have stayed down. But Jim scrambled to his feet, rolled right, and threw a scoring pass to tight end Pete Metzelaars in the deep corner of the end zone. The kick brought the bills to 28–24 with 3:55 left.

Unfortunately, the Buffalo defense couldn't get the ball back. The Jets won the game. But Jim had shocked everyone with a 20-of-33 performance, good for 292 yards and three touchdowns. He wasn't intercepted and was sacked just one time.

Joe Klecko, an All-Pro New York defender, was full of praise for Kelly. "I didn't think he'd be this tough," Klecko said. "If he was hurt, he sure didn't show it. He's heady, too. He's got quicker moves than you think."

It didn't take Jim long to fit in with his new team. In fact, he even surprised himself.

"I knew I was going to get hit a lot," he said, "but I also got hit a lot playing for the Gamblers. For some reason, I felt more relaxed here than in the USFL. I felt at home. I want to win for the people here. I've just got the taste of winning so bad in my mouth right now."

Winning would have to wait a bit. Despite Jim's consistently fine play all year, the Bills only managed a 4-12 record. In midseason the team made a coaching change, with Marv Levy taking over for Hank Bullough. But it was still a matter of the defense having to catch up with the offense. For Jim Kelly was outstanding. He completed 285 of 480 passes for 3,593 yards and a 59.4 completion percentage. Despite the team's poor record, he tossed 22 touchdown passes and was intercepted just 17 times.

A year later the team improved to 7-8. It was the year of the players' strike, and the season was just 15 games. Jim played in only 12 games, but was outstanding again. There was little question that he had arrived.

During the season he was twice named AFC Offensive Player of the Week, had a streak of 141 passes without an interception, and when the season ended was selected to play in his first Pro Bowl. He had proven that his two record-setting years in the USFL were no fluke. Jim Kelly was a superstar in any league.

A year later the entire Bills team arrived. There was more balance on both offense and defense. Rookie running back Thurman Thomas was equally adept as a runner or receiver out of the backfield. Wideout Andre Reed was an All-Pro, and the offen-

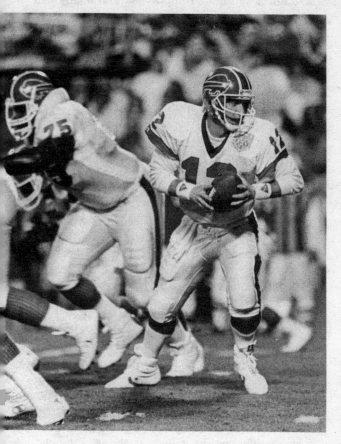

Jim was outstanding from his first game with the Bills. Here he turns to hand the ball off to one of his running backs.

(Vernon J. Biever Photo)

sive line was big and improving. Jim finally had the right tools.

Defensively, the team had made giant strides. Defensive end Bruce Smith and linebacker Cornelius Bennett were among the best at their positions. Linebackers Darryl Talley and Shane Conlan teamed with Bennett to give the Bills one of the best groups in the league. The rest of the line and defensive secondary was also steady.

Still, no one expected the kind of turnaround the Bills produced in 1988. With the defense having an outstanding year, Buffalo won the AFC East with a 12-4 record. They won their share of low-scoring games, taking victories by scores of 13–10, 9–6, 16–14, 13–3, and 9–6 again. But they also erupted several times, winning by scores of 36–28, 34–23, 31–6, and 37–21. After 12 games the team was 11-1 and being called by some the league's best. But they lost three of their last four, derailing the express somewhat.

Jim started all 16 games. He threw for 3,380 yards, completing 59.5 percent of his passes. His TD tosses were down to 15 and his intercepts up to 17. The team didn't have real instant striking power, and some said they depended too much on their swarming, talented defense.

In the playoffs the club put forth a solid, workmanlike effort in beating Houston, 17–10. Jim completed 19 of 33 passes for 244 yards. But the game plan was conservative and he failed to throw a touchdown pass. That approach caught up with the Bills in the AFC title game with Cincinnati. One step away from the Super Bowl, the offense sputtered.

Jim completed just 14 of 30 passes for 163 yards. Playing from behind most of the way, he was intercepted three times and the Bills failed to convert on a single third-down play all afternoon. The 21–10 loss was a bitter disappointment after a surprisingly successful season. Coach Levy promised to retune his offense for 1989.

The result was a strange season. The offense exploded out of the blocks, and the defense seemed to fall back a notch. Explain that. But during the first half of the season the Bills were one of the highest scoring teams in the league.

"We've caught the scoring bug," Jim said, "and I love it."

In the opener, Jim dove across the goal line with no time left on the clock to give the Bills a 27–24 comeback win over the Dolphins. Then in the third game of the season, the Bills beat Houston, 47–41, in an offensive slugfest.

Jim missed three games in the middle of the season with a separated left shoulder. Frank Reich came on and proved he was an extremely able backup. Jim returned and continued to lead the offense.

"I think I'm playing as well as I ever have," he said. "People ask me now if I think I belong with the top quarterbacks in football, and I tell them I think I've belonged from Day One. I'm not going to say I'm the best quarterback in the league, but I'm definitely in the top three."

Confidence was not something that Jim Kelly lacked. Give him the ball in any circumstance and he felt he could get the job done. Late in the season, however, the team lost four of five games and had to blow out the New York Jets, 37–0, in the final game to clinch the AFC East at 9-7.

Jim played in 13 games in 1989, throwing for 3,130

yards and a 58.3 completion percentage. His TD passes were back up to 25, while he had 18 picked off. Thurman Thomas ran for 1,244 yards and caught 60 passes for 669 more. He had the most total yards from scrimmage of any back in the league and scored 12 touchdowns. Andre Reed caught 88 passes for 1,312 yards and nine TDs.

It appeared that the Bills had a good chance in the playoffs: Jim had perhaps his best season; the offense had the potential to explode. If the defense could come up big, the team could very well be headed for the Super Bowl. But the dream ended quickly.

The Bills drew first blood against the Cleveland Browns when Jim hit Andre Reed with a 72-yard touchdown bomb in the first period. But by halftime the Browns had a 17–14 lead. Cleveland outplayed the Bills in the third and early in the fourth periods. With 6:50 left in the game, the Browns had a 10-point lead at 34–24.

Jim then put the ball in the air 23 straight times. With four minutes left he hit Thomas in the end zone from the three. The point was missed but the gap was now 4, at 34–30. In the closing seconds the Bills were driving again. With just nine seconds left on the clock, Buffalo had the ball at the Cleveland 11 and Jim dropped back again. He looked toward the goal line and fired. Browns' linebacker Clay Matthews stepped into the path of the ball and picked it off. The Bills were beaten by a whisker, 34–30.

Jim had made a valiant effort. He completed 28 of 54 passes for 405 yards and four touchdowns. Two of his passes were picked off, including the final one. So despite his efforts, the season ended in disappointment.

Then came 1990 and the Bills really came of age. During the regular season the team was a juggernaut. With veteran wide receiver James Lofton making a brilliant comeback, the Bills had another offensive weapon to go with Kelly, Thomas, and Reed. And as good as the team was all year, they unveiled another unique strategy late in the season: the no-huddle offense.

The offense doesn't gather in the traditional huddle to plan the next play. Rather, they just line up with the quarterback usually in the shotgun, calling out the play, and go. The Bills began using it on every series and taking opposing defenses by surprise. Jim Kelly loved it.

"It's the ultimate," Jim said. "A quarterback shouldn't want it any other way. I want to take the risks, the extra gamble, and this is the way I can do it."

The Bills finished the season at 13-3, averaging a league-best 26.7 points per game. Jim was the league's highest rated passer with a 101.3 rating, just the fifth quarterback to have a 100-plus rating. He completed a career-best 63.3 percent of his passes, throwing for 2,829 yards with 24 touchdowns and only nine interceptions. The Washington Touchdown Club named him NFL Player of the Year, and he was an All-Pro.

Jim had missed the final two games of the regular season with a knee injury but returned for the AFC divisional playoff against Miami. He led the Bills to a 44–34 victory over the Dolphins. Now the Bills were in the AFC title game against the Los Angeles Raiders. Once again they were one step away from the Super Bowl.

The game against the Raiders was over almost before it began. Just three and a half minutes into the first period, Jim hit James Lofton with a 13-yard TD pass and the rout was on. The final score was 51–3—the largest margin of victory in club history. Jim was 17 of 23 for 300 yards and two scores. But he had help from everyone.

The Bills were on their way to the Super Bowl, where they would be meeting perhaps the one team that had the style to beat them—the New York Giants. That didn't bother Jim or any of his teammates.

"I have the weapons," Jim said. "And when I have the weapons and the time, I don't think anybody can stop us."

But the Giants had two things going for them. On offense they were a ball-control team that liked to run and throw short, keeping the football for long, time-consuming drives. If they could do that, they would keep Jim and the no-huddle offense off the field. They also had a punishing, rock-ribbed defense led by all-world linebacker Lawrence Taylor.

Super Bowl XXV was played at Tampa Stadium in Florida on January 27, 1991, and it proved to be one of the best title games ever. It was close all the way. After the two teams traded field goals, the Bills scored early in the second period to take a 10–3 lead. Minutes later they had the ball again and began to move. But a dropped third-down pass stopped the drive.

"I thought we were in control at that point," Jim said. "We were moving the ball well and if we scored on that drive, we had a chance to blow the game open. But I made a bad read of the defense on that third-down play and then there were some dropped passes.''

When Bruce Smith tackled the Giants' Jeff Hostetler in the end zone for a safety, the lead was 12–3. But the Giants scored with less than a minute remaining in the half to make it 12–10. In the third period the Giants began controlling the ball. Ottis Anderson scored on a one-yard run with about 2:30 remaining in the session and the Giants had a 17–12 lead.

Buffalo came right back. They went 63 yards on four plays for the score. Scott Norwood's kick made it a 19–17 game, Buffalo in front. But then the Giants began another long, ball-control drive. Their last score had come on a 14-play drive, and so was this one. When it stalled at the 4, Matt Bahr kicked a 21-yard field goal to give the Giants a 20–19 lead.

The Bills had their final chance with just 2:16 left in the game. They began at the Giants' 10, and in eight plays traveled 16 yards to the Giants' 29-yard line. There were eight seconds left on the clock when Scott Norwood came out to try a 47-yard field goal.

Football fans all over the country sat on the edge of their seats as Norwood stepped forward and booted the ball. It was high enough, deep enough, but at the last second it faded off to the right and missed the uprights by about a foot. No good. The Giants had won, 20–19.

It was a devastating loss for the Bills. The Giants had done the one thing they had to do—their offense held the ball for a Super Bowl–record 40 minutes and 33 seconds. That meant Jim and his offense had less than 20 minutes to put points on the board. Jim praised the Giants but felt he and his offense could still have won it.

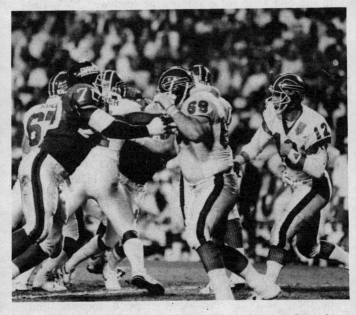

Jim played an outstanding game when the Bills met the Giants in the Super Bowl. He shows almost perfect form as he completes a pass against the ferocious New York defense.

(Vernon J. Biever Photo)

Despite the loss, the Bills had proved a great deal in 1990 and proved it again in 1991. Once again they won the AFC East, with another 13-3 record. Jim played in 15 games and produced another All-Pro year. He was the top AFC passer, with a 97.6 rating, completing a career-high 304 passes for a career-best 3,844 yards. He had his best completion percentage, 64.1, and threw for 33 touchdowns, another personal high.

In the opening round of the playoffs, Buffalo whipped Kansas City, 37-14, as Jim threw for 273 yards. The AFC title game against Denver was much closer. Jim and his offense couldn't get on track, but the defense came up big in a 10–7 squeaker. Jim was just 13 of 25 for 117 yards. Now the team was headed for a second straight Super Bowl. This time they would be meeting the Washington Redskins, considered by many the best team in football.

Unfortunately, this one wasn't close. The Bills lost 37–24. The Redskin defense shut down the Buffalo running game early and Jim was forced to throw 58 times, a Super Bowl record, completing 28 for 275 yards and two scores. But he was intercepted four times and sacked on five occasions. He didn't want to throw that much, but playing from behind, with the running game shut down, will do that. The question now was whether the team could continue to play at a high level. Two Super Bowl losses can make it difficult.

The Bills remained one of the NFL's upper-echelon teams in 1992. Despite injuries to key players, the team had a solid year. They finished at 11-5, same as the Dolphins in the AFC East, but Miami was given the division title based on the NFL tie-breaking system.

Still, the Bills were the highest scoring team in the AFC, though most experts felt the team wouldn't get very far in the playoffs.

Jim finished as the fourth leading passer in the AFC, but his numbers were down from the two previous seasons. Still running the no-huddle, he threw for 3,457 yards, with a 58.2 completion percentage and 23 touchdowns. He also finished the season with a knee injury that would keep him out of the wild-card playoff game. Backup Frank Reich became the starter.

The game against Houston became a classic. The Oilers came out of the gate on fire and the Bills reacted like a beaten team. It was 28–3 at the half. Then on the first drive of the third quarter, a Reich pass was tipped and intercepted by Bubba McDowell, who raced 58 yards for another Houston score. The kick made it 35–3, and the obits for the Bills were underway.

Then something happened. Reich led the Bills on a 50-yard drive, Davis scoring from the one. Minutes later Reich hit Don Beebe for a 38-yard score. Then it was Reed, on the end of a 26-yard scoring strike from Reich. Minutes later Reed caught an 18-yarder for yet another score. Suddenly it was a 35–31 game going into the fourth quarter.

Buffalo miraculously took the lead in the fourth, only to have an Oiler field goal tie the game at 38–all. Then, just over three minutes into overtime, the Bills' Steve Christie booted a 32-yard field goal to win it, 41–38. The Bills had just completed the greatest comeback in NFL history.

A week later they made it look much easier, topping the Pittsburgh Steelers 24–3, as Frank Reich again starred by hitting 16 of 23 passes, good for 160 yards and two touchdowns. Suddenly the Bills were Super Bowl contenders again, preparing to meet Miami for the AFC championship. Coach Levy answered the big question, Who would quarterback his team?

"If Jim Kelly is able to play, he'll start, period," said Levy.

The week of the game Jim's knee appeared better. He tried several braces to stabilize the knee.

"Any time you get an injury you're a little leary about moving certain ways," he said. "But as practice wore on, it started feeling more comfortable. By the end of practice, I was almost doing things and not even thinking about it [the knee]."

The game was played at Joe Robbie Stadium in Miami. Sure enough, Jim was on the field and ready for action. Many felt that Buffalo should have stayed with Frank Reich. The fans had even voted, and the majority wanted Reich. But Reich deferred to Jim, saying he was more than willing to resume his backup role.

The pressure, therefore, was squarely on Jim Kelly's shoulders. Had he been overanxious or impatient, he might have tried to do too much himself. That's something he admits to doing in the past. He said he also learned the value of patience by watching Frank Reich the past two weeks.

After an exchange of field goals in the first quarter, Jim really got the Bills moving in the second. He led the team on a 64-yard drive in seven plays, ending it with a 17-yard touchdown strike to Thurman Thomas. The extra point and a Steve Christie field goal later in the period made it 13–3 at the half.

The Bills recovered a fumble of the opening second-half kickoff and Jim drove them 24 yards for another score. That made it 20–3. They continued to control the ball and the offense. Buffalo finally won the game, 29–10. The Bills were headed to the Super Bowl for a third straight year.

Jim was a very consistent 17 of 24 for 177 yards. He had done just what he wanted to—played within himself and exhibited patience.

"I know we have one more game to go," he said afterward. "But right now this is the biggest win of my life." Someone asked if it was because of the pressure on him, and Jim answered quickly, "Yes."

So the Bills headed to the Rose Bowl in Pasadena, California. Their third try for a Super Bowl crown would be against the young Dallas Cowboys, who had vanquished the mighty San Francisco 49ers in the NFC title game. Dallas was made the early favorite. Having lost the last two Super Bowls, the pressure was squarely on the Bills.

Everyone, including Jim, felt the team was ready. When Steve Tasker blocked a punt early in the first quarter, Jim drove the Bills for a quick touchdown and a 7–0 lead. But after that, the team self-destructed in a rash of nine turnovers. Jim threw two early interceptions and lost a fumble inside his own five that led to a Dallas score.

Then early in the second quarter, he was blindsided by Dallas linebacker Ken Norton, Jr., a hit that reinjured his knee and caused him to leave the game. He had completed four of seven passes at the time of the injury. Frank Reich came on but couldn't get the team moving either. Dallas rolled over the Bills, 52–17, handing Buffalo yet another Super Bowl loss.

It was a bitter loss for Jim and his teammates. "You think, why? Why do we deserve to lose the way we did today?" Jim asked after the game. "Everybody was out there giving 100 percent. It hurts emotionally more than it does physically. It's not a good feeling."

It won't be easy to forget. Jim and his teammates will need all the toughness they can muster. But like all real competitors, they will enter the next season determined to do it again. Their goal, like all other teams, will be to reach the Super Bowl. For Jim Kelly has never considered himself a loser. And neither have the rest of the Buffalo Bills.

BERNIE KOSAR

THE MAJORITY OF THE MODERN-DAY NATIONAL FOOT-
ball League quarterbacks come from a similar mold.
While all are individuals in mind and temperament,
they are similar physically. The modern quarterback
is usually big and strong, well over six feet tall and
very athletic. Most of them move very well and can
escape a pass rush.

All of today's quarterbacks have rockets for arms
and can whistle a pass downfield with seeming ease.
They deliver the ball in a classic, overhand style so
they can throw over the outstretched arms of tall
charging linemen.

But one top quarterback is different. He's Bernie
Kosar of the Cleveland Browns. Kosar is tall (6′5″)
and weighs some 215 pounds. But that's where his
resemblance to other NFL signal callers ends. Kosar
is slow. He has next to no speed to avoid a pass rush
and readily admits it. He's almost never a threat to
take off and run. Nor does he have a super strong

Bernie Kosar can always manage a smile when he's ready to play quarterback. A love of the game and desire to improve have always given Bernie a positive outlook.

(Courtesy Cleveland Browns)

arm. He doesn't deliver the ball in the classic overhand motion. More often he throws the ball sidearm, the way quarterbacks *aren't* supposed to throw.

In an age when many college athletes have to struggle to graduate because their sport demands so much of their time, Bernie Kosar earned enough credits to graduate before his class at the University of Miami. Consequently he became the youngest starting quarterback in the National Football League when he took over the helm of the Cleveland Browns in 1985. At that time Bernie Kosar was just 21 years old.

Kosar has not only survived, he's prospered. His keen football intelligence enabled him to learn the pro game quickly. While he has never taken the Browns to the Super Bowl, he has had his club in the AFC title game three times.

Because the Browns have been down the last couple of years, Bernie has had to stand up to a ferocious pass rush and has taken a pounding resulting in several injuries. But as the team rebuilds under new coach Bill Belichick, Kosar is still ticketed as the man to lead the Browns' offense. Confidence in Bernie's unique though unorthodox abilities has never wavered. Not an inch.

Bernie Kosar, Jr., was born in Boardman, Ohio, on November 25, 1963. He was the eldest of Bernie Sr. and Geri Kosar's three children. All three—Bernie, his brother, Brian, and sister, Beth—had strong family values and excelled academically, always doing more than they had to.

"We always wanted our kids to do whatever they enjoyed," Geri Kosar said. "If it was sports, fine. We wanted them tired and out of trouble. We always knew where they were at ten o'clock at night—in bed, asleep."

Mr. Kosar was an industrial engineer, but when U.S. Steel closed its Youngstown, Ohio, operation in 1980, he began a career as an air-compressor salesman. He didn't want to move his family from Boardman. He felt it was a good place to raise his children, even if it meant a career change. Mrs. Kosar worked as a registered nurse.

There was always a lot of sports action around the Kosar home. Mr. Kosar's sports advice to the boys was "If it feels good, do it." He never pushed them, but encouraged them to play hard whenever they played. In addition, both Mr. and Mrs. Kosar stressed academics—they wanted well-rounded children capable of making mature decisions about their futures.

When Bernie came home after his second day in the first grade he told his parents he didn't like it and wasn't going back.

"They still haven't taught me to read," the impatient youngster said.

While he encouraged sports, Mr. Kosar believed that youngsters shouldn't be forced into structured programs too early. He didn't let young Bernie play organized football until he was in the seventh grade.

By the time Bernie was playing Little League baseball he had already developed the kind of drive that all successful athletes have. His technique, however, was another story. They couldn't get him to throw over the top even then.

"We worked and worked on it when he was pitching during Little League," said his father. "We tried to stretch that long body over the top. But he was so effective throwing the way he did, usually from three-quarters, that you just hated to tamper with anything."

His father remembers a Little League championship game when Bernie was nine.

"All the other kids were 10, 11, or 12," Mr. Kosar said. "They brought Bernie in from second base to pitch the last inning, and he struck out the side to win the game for his team. I remember the look of determination he had on his face. It was something he kept right into the pros."

Like many top athletes, Bernie played football,

baseball, and basketball. He was a three-sport star at Boardman High School. His favorite player at that time was Cleveland Browns quarterback Brian Sipe. Cleveland was just 60 miles from Boardman, and Bernie was an avid Browns fan.

Brian Sipe wasn't especially big or strong, and he didn't have the proverbial cannon for an arm. But he knew how to run a passing game, and he had some big years for the Browns. Not surprisingly, the brainy Kosar appreciated the way Sipe played the game and how he used his talents to the maximum.

At Boardman High, Bernie was the quarterback of the football team, a forward with the basketball squad, and third baseman on the baseball team. No one complained about those three-quarter and side-arm throws from third as long as the ball got to first before the runner. They usually did.

Bernie's football career at Boardman didn't take off instantly. He was injured most of his sophomore season and saw little action. As a junior he and all his teammates were affected by a school strike. So entering his senior season, 1981, he was not one of the nation's hot prospects. In fact, none of the colleges really knew about him.

Playing his entire senior year, Bernie did everything he could to make people take notice, though he was just trying to win football games. He passed for 2,222 yards and 19 touchdowns while leading his team to a fine 8-2 record. For his efforts he was named Ohio Player of the Year by the Associated Press. Yet despite his success, the major colleges close to Boardman didn't consider him a big-time prospect.

Fortunately for Bernie, there was a coach and a school that saw the potential in the tall, gangly high-school quarterback—the University of Miami. The football team was coached by Howard Schnellenberger, an exponent of a pro-type passing game.

The year that Coach Schnellenberger recruited Bernie Kosar his team already had an outstanding strong-armed quarterback named Jim Kelly. Kelly would be a senior in 1982, Bernie's freshman year. So if Bernie was good enough, he would have the opportunity to take over for Kelly in 1983, which would be his sophomore season. It seemed like a perfect match.

Bernie arrived at Miami in the fall of 1982 and shortly afterward the decision was made to redshirt him that year. He wouldn't be part of the team except for practice; therefore, he would be eligible to play for another four years after that. The thinking was that Bernie wouldn't play much with Kelly on board anyway. What no one counted on was Jim Kelly's going down in the third game with a serious shoulder injury that would finish him for the year.

Bernie learned a great deal about the Miami offense by working with quarterback coach Marc Trestman after hours. The two would talk football and go over the Miami offense. Trestman was amazed at how easily the 18-year-old Kosar picked up the game.

"I could see then that his aptitude for the finer points of the game was simply awesome," said Trestman. "Bernie's just smarter than anybody else, that's all."

In 1983 Kelly was gone and Bernie was still officially a freshman quarterback. He was ready to lead the team and quickly won the job before the season opener.

The Hurricanes had a very solid team in 1983. Running backs Alonzo Highsmith and Melvin Bratton were outstanding, while Eddie Brown was a great deep receiver. So the offense was in capable hands. But the opener would be a tough one. The Hurricanes would be visiting archrival Florida State, and the freshman quarterback would have to deal with some 74,000 fans rooting against him.

It was a game that could have shattered the confidence of even veteran quarterbacks, let alone a 19-year-old starting in his first game. It was also a game that could have destroyed the team's faith in its young quarterback. Despite disastrous results, it did neither. If anything, the Miami team became convinced that Bernie Kosar was their man.

Florida dominated from the start. And just when it looked as if the Hurricanes would rally, the Gators came up with another big play. They took the lead early and kept extending it. The final was 28–3, which makes it sound like a real disaster for Miami. But a closer look tells another story.

For openers, Bernie tied a Miami record set by George Mira back in the early 1960s when he completed 25 passes in a losing cause. He wasn't intimidated by the score or the opposition in his first taste of varsity action. He also showed his toughness when he was hit hard by several Gator defenders and wobbled to the sideline, dazed and dizzy. Coach Schnellenberger was about to send another quarterback into the game when Bernie said, "Where are the smelling salts? Those guys aren't going to put me out of the game."

When the game ended, Coach Schnellenberger had nothing but praise for his team and its young quarterback.

"It's easy to show poise when you win," the coach

said. "It's tougher when you're getting your rear end kicked in front of 74,000 fanatics. We came out of that game a lot more confident than before."

Schnellenberger was right. The Hurricanes began to win, and Bernie Kosar was looking more and more like a confident and winning quarterback. Suddenly Miami appeared to be one of the best teams in the country. Bernie's teammates, especially his offensive line, admired his courage and leadership.

One of them, Alvin Ward, spoke for most of his teammates when he said he was "prepared to die for Bernie."

After the opening loss to Florida State, the Hurricanes won 10 straight to finish the season at 10-1. The Associated Press had the Hurricanes ranked number five in the country, while United Press had them in the four spot.

As for Bernie, he had completed 201 of 327 passes for 2,329 yards and 15 touchdowns. His completion percentage was 61.5, and he had just 13 passes intercepted. It was quite a record for a freshman quarterback, and it wasn't over yet. The Hurricanes had received a bid to play in the Orange Bowl against the unbeaten number-one ranked team, Nebraska. The Cornhuskers were 11-point favorites to beat Miami.

Not at all intimidated by playing the nation's top team in the Orange Bowl, Bernie went to work. In the first quarter he threw touchdown passes of two and 22 yards to Glenn Dennison. Sandwiched in between was a 45-yard field goal by Jeff Davis, and the 'Canes took a 17–0 first period lead.

Nebraska wasn't unbeaten for nothing. The Cornhuskers came back to narrow the margin to 17–14 at the half. A field goal early in the third period tied it at 17. In the third period, Kosar led the 'Canes on two long drives resulting in touchdowns that made the score 31–17. Nebraska then scored to make it 31–24 and with time running down began driving again.

With just 48 seconds left, Nebraska's Jeff Smith ran 24 yards for another score. That made it 31–30 with the all-important extra point coming up. Tom Osborne, the Nebraska coach, elected to go for a two-point conversion and the win. Quarterback Turner Gill tried to hit Smith in the end zone, but defensive back Ken Calhoun knocked the ball away. Miami had won it by a point.

Bernie was brilliant again. He completed 19 of 35 passes for an Orange Bowl–record 300 yards and two scores. He was named the game's Most Valuable Player for his efforts. That wasn't all. Second-ranked Texas lost to Georgia in the Cotton Bowl and Illinois, ranked ahead of Miami in the AP poll, lost to UCLA in the Rose Bowl. At the same time, number three Auburn won in the Sugar Bowl but could manage just three field goals. When the final polls were released, Miami was on top of both.

The Hurricanes were national champions, and freshman Bernie Kosar was the toast of the town.

"Nine out of 10 times he threw to the right man," Coach Schnellenberger said. "That's not 75 percent. That's 90 percent, and that is amazing."

During the off-season Bernie tried to stay out of the limelight, something that would become a trademark. "I'd rather just blend in," he once said. "It's impossible because I'm the quarterback, I know. But I'd like to."

So Bernie simply took more classes. He had a double major in economics and finance and a 3.4 grade-

point average and he didn't want to waste time. As
Bernie got ready for his sophomore season, Howard
Schnellenberger had left and Jimmy Johnson was the
new Miami coach. Johnson was also committed to
the same kind of passing game, and he built his offense around the talents of Bernie Kosar.

It was an offense that often sent three receivers
flooding into a zone protected by only a pair of defenders. It was then up to the quarterback to make a
quick read and throw to the open man. That's what
Coach Schnellenberger had meant when he said that
Bernie threw to the right man 90 percent of the time.

The 1984 Hurricanes weren't as well balanced as
the previous year's club, but they were still dangerous, especially with Bernie Kosar throwing the football. It wasn't long before the records began falling
again. Against Maryland, Bernie set a new school
mark with 30 completions. Then in a game with Cincinnati, he fired five touchdown passes for another
school mark, including an 85-yarder to Eddie Brown.
He was averaging some 300 passing yards per game.

The Hurricanes wouldn't be national champs in
1984, but they played in one classic game that will
always be remembered. Bernie Kosar was at the center of the action, along with another top collegiate
quarterback in 1984, Doug Flutie of Boston College.

Flutie had captured the public's imagination because he was just 5'9½", very small for a big-time
quarterback. Yet he was effective, a scrambler who
could throw on the run or from the pocket. Like
Kosar, he had a feel for the passing game and was
putting big numbers on the board week after week.
The game was played on November 23 and scheduled
for national television. It was billed as a shootout

between two of college football's top quarterbacks. It didn't disappoint.

The game was played on a soggy field at the Orange Bowl in Miami. Flutie set the tone early, putting the ball in the air with a 33-yard scoring pass and giving his team the early 7–0 lead. The two clubs then traded touchdowns, and at the end of one period it was a 14–7 game, the Eagles leading.

Bernie led the Hurricanes on two long drives in the second period, mixing his passes with slashing runs by Melvin Bratton. Both drives resulted in scores. But in between Flutie had scored on a nine-yard scramble, and at the end of the half he hit Gerard Phelan from 10 yards out to keep his team in the lead, 28–21.

After Miami tied it in the third, the two clubs traded field goals. Another field goal early in the fourth quarter put BC on top, 34–31. But then Bratton electrified the home fans with a broken-field, 52-yard touchdown run that gave Miami the lead once again, 38–34. Now it was Flutie's turn. He drove his club downfield and then gave it to Steve Strachan, who scored from the one. The kick put the Eagles in front once again, 41–38.

With time running down, Bernie started throwing into the heart of the Eagles' defense. Neither defense could stop these two daring passers. Finally he drove the team inside the 10, then to the one. From there, Melvin Bratton took it over for his fourth score. The kick made it a 45–41 game with just 28 seconds left. It looked like an amazing finish.

But was it over? After the kickoff, Flutie knew he'd have to get his team into the end zone. Miami went into a prevent defense to stop the long gainer.

Flutie threw underneath the coverage and got his team to the Miami 48. But now there was time for just one more play. Everyone knew what Flutie had to do. He put three receivers on the right side of the field and at the snap sent all three toward the end zone. Flutie dropped back, waited, then threw the ball high and deep, more than 60 yards in the air, toward the end zone.

More than half a dozen players from both teams went up for the ball. It was batted into the air and suddenly someone grabbed it. Flutie began jumping in the air. So did the Boston College bench. For there was Gerard Phelan clutching the football. He had grabbed the deflection. Boston College had a miracle touchdown. They had won the game, 47–45, as Flutie's dramatic "Hail Mary" pass became part of college football legend.

It was a crushing loss for Miami, but what a great game it had been. Flutie had completed 34 of 46 passes for 472 yards and three touchdowns. Bernie wasn't far behind. He had thrown the football 38 times, completing 25 for 447 yards and a pair of scores. The game was talked about from coast to coast, with accolades for both quarterbacks.

Bernie finished the regular season with 262 completions on 416 attempts for 3,642 yards and 25 touchdowns. He had a completion percentage of 63.0 and had 16 passes pilfered. He was named a second-team All-American by the Associated Press and was a first-team Academic All-American. Against UCLA in the Fiesta Bowl, he completed 31 of 44 passes for 294 yards and two scores. He seemed to be getting better and better, and he was still only a sophomore.

In just two years, Bernie had thrown for 5,971

Always dangerous late in a game, Bernie excelled in the clutch at the University of Miami and also with the Browns. He is considered one of the smartest quarterbacks in the game.

(Courtesy Cleveland Browns)

yards and 40 scores. He had completed 62.3 percent of his passes and had set 22 Miami passing records. But there was a problem. Bernie had taken so many extra courses that he was due to graduate with a BA in economics and finance the following June. Yet he still had two years of football eligibility remaining.

Bernie Kosar suddenly had a very big decision to make: to play for Miami the next season or in the NFL. Because he didn't want to keep Coach Johnson and the team hanging, he had to make it quickly. If he stayed to play football, he kiddingly said he'd have a Ph.D. before he was through. But perhaps more than anything else, he was beginning to find college ball boring.

"College football was no longer challenging," he said. "With our passing system at Miami, which was head and shoulders above any other college's, after a while it was just too easy. For me to continue to grow at so slow a pace—what was the point?"

That was probably the real reason for Bernie Kosar's decision. Why not move on? He felt ready, so in March he announced he would be leaving the University of Miami and entering the 1985 supplemental draft. He would play in the National Football League in the fall of 1985.

There was a lot of grousing from Miami fans. Some felt Bernie was running out with two years of eligibility left.

"I always thought the object of going to college was to graduate," he said. "And I'm graduating in June."

He also made no secret of where he wanted to play: "All my life I've dreamed of playing for the Cleveland Browns," he said.

That was surprising, since the Browns seemed to be a team in decline. In 1984 Cleveland finished with a dismal 5-11 record.

But there was a great football tradition on the shores of Lake Erie. This was where the Hall of Fame quarterback Otto Graham played. And this was where Jim Brown made his reputation as the greatest running back of all time. But that was only part of why Bernie wanted to play there. To him, Cleveland was home, and there would be nothing better than to have a pro career at home. Browns' owner Art Modell was among those who were surprised and impressed when they heard the news.

"It's not every day that somebody *wants* to play in Cleveland," Modell said. "This has already lent such an aura to Bernie."

To get Kosar, the Browns had to make a deal with the Buffalo Bills, who had the first choice. They gave the Bills four draft choices, including a pair of number ones. That was how badly they wanted Bernie. Once they picked him they quickly signed him to a five-year, five-million-dollar contract. Bernie said right away there wouldn't be fancy sports cars or gold chains in his immediate future.

"I just want to give my family the security they've always given me," he said.

When Bernie joined the team, the Browns' quarterback situation was unsettled. During the off-season the team had acquired veteran Gary Danielson from Detroit. But Danielson had never been a full-fledged star and was often beset with a variety of injuries. So the door seemed open for Bernie Kosar, though he was still only 21 years old when he joined the Browns for his first NFL training camp.

Bernie made his pro debut in the second preseason game, against the Philadelphia Eagles. He was slated to play the first half, and a large crowd showed up at Cleveland's Municipal Stadium to watch the rookie perform. The results were mixed.

There were some bright spots. Early in the second quarter he completed two straight impressive passes. But three plays later he tried to scramble and wound up fumbling the ball away. All in all, he was 6 of 22 for 97 yards. His coach, Marty Schottenheimer, said he saw Bernie's potential.

"Bernie has a presence out there," said the coach. "You can tell he's going to be an outstanding player in this league. The game tonight simply illustrates the difference between college football and the NFL."

There was also concern about Bernie's physical shortcomings, his lack of speed and the way in which he threw the football. He joked about some of the criticisms.

"When I run," he said, "I'm not in a hurry."

Gary Danielson was named the starter and took all the snaps in the first four games of the 1985 season. The team won two and lost two. Coming off a 5-11 season, the Browns were hoping to get back into play-off contention. So it wasn't a bad start. Then late in the second quarter of the fifth game, against New England, Danielson was injured. He was hit hard and the result was a separated shoulder.

Suddenly Bernie Kosar was in the game. He took his first regular-season NFL snap with 2:12 remaining in the half—and fumbled it! But shortly after that, the real Bernie Kosar stood up. He completed his first six passes and, with the Browns trailing 20–17 in the final period, led his team on a long touchdown drive to win the game, 24–20. Bernie was 9 of 15 for 105 yards in his first taste of action. With Danielson out, the job was now his.

Fortunately, the Browns had a two-pronged running attack in 1985. Both Earnest Byner and Kevin Mack were on a 1,000-yard pace, and Bernie could rely on them for long, sustained touchdown drives. He also had an outstanding receiver in tight end Ozzie Newsome, and another good one in Brian Brennan. But that first year he didn't have too many real big passing days. Against Cincinnati he completed 16 of 32 for 229 yards, and against Seattle he connected on 18 of 31 for 249 yards. When the season ended, the Browns had made the playoffs as a wild card at 8-8. Bernie didn't have great numbers, but he was proving himself a winner.

He completed 124 of 248 passes for 1,578 yards, 8 touchdowns, and 7 interceptions. At one point he threw 134 passes without an interception.

In the playoffs the Browns were beaten by the Miami Dolphins, 24–21. There were some who felt he wasn't the kind of passer the team needed, that he was always going to be a Punch-and-Judy quarterback, throwing short passes and not excelling without a powerful running game. Yet just one year later he made all the critics eat their words.

With a pair of speedy wide receivers in Webster Slaughter and Reggie Langhorne joining forces with Brennan and Newsome, Bernie had more options on the passing game. Both Byner and Mack were also fine receivers out of the backfield. Even though the club lost two of its first three games, it was obviously a different Bernie Kosar at the helm.

Against Chicago in the opener, Bernie completed

23 of 40 for 289 yards, and against Cincinnati in game three, he was 28 of 40 for 293 yards. In that one he completed 70 percent of his passes. After that the team began to win. In fact, they lost just two more games over the remainder of the season, as Bernie Kosar emerged as an outstanding quarterback and leader.

His biggest game was a 28-for-46, 414-yard performance against Pittsburgh, a 37–31 overtime win in which he threw for two scores. He also threw for 401 yards against the Miami Dolphins and led his team to another overtime win against Houston. In the final game of the season, against San Diego, he completed 21 of 28 passes for 258 yards and 2 scores. The Browns won, 47–17, as Bernie completed 75 percent of his tosses.

The team finished the regular season as AFC Central champs at 12–4, the most wins in club history. Bernie completed 310 of 531 passes for 3,854 yards, 17 touchdowns, and just 10 interceptions. His completion percentage was 58.4. He had the lowest interception percentage of any quarterback in the league, and at one point he threw 171 straight passes without a pickoff.

In the divisional playoffs, the Browns would be meeting the New York Jets. The Jets scored first, but Bernie answered with a 37-yard TD toss to running back Herman Fontenot. An exchange of field goals made it a 10–10 game at the half. The Jets took a 13–10 lead after three quarters, then made it 20–10 with just 4:14 remaining in the game. It looked as if the Browns were done.

But Bernie wouldn't quit. He was brilliant in leading his team on a 68-yard touchdown drive. The kick made it 20–17 with just 1:57 left. Then the Cleveland defense forced a punt with just 51 seconds left. Bernie quickly drove his team to the Jets' 42, then completed a 37-yard pass to Slaughter. With just seconds left, Mark Moseley booted the field goal to send it into overtime.

Neither team could score in the first OT period, so they went to a second. Bernie brought his team downfield to the nine, and Moseley came on to kick a 27-yard field goal to win it, 23–20. Bernie had completed 33 of 64 passes for a whopping 489 yards. The Browns were in the AFC title game against Denver, just a step away from the Super Bowl.

It was another incredible game. With Kosar squaring off against Denver's explosive quarterback, John Elway, the fans got their money's worth. The game was hard fought and tied at 13–13 in the fourth quarter. Then, with just under six minutes left and the ball at the Denver 48, Bernie whipped a pass to Brian Brennan, who took it into the end zone for the go-ahead score. The kick made it 20–13, Cleveland.

The Broncos bobbled the kickoff and had to start from their own two-yard line with 5:32 left. Elway then proceeded to lead a long, time-consuming march that resulted in the tying touchdown. It will be forever remembered as The Drive. It sent the game into overtime. That was when Bernie and the Browns ran out of miracles. Cleveland stalled, and Elway drove his team to the 15, allowing Rich Karlis to boot the winning field goal. The Browns had lost a heartbreaker, 23–20.

No one could fault Bernie Kosar. He had completed 18 of 32 passes for 259 yards, a pair of scores and two interceptions. He proved that he belonged among the NFL's quarterback elite. The Browns' executive vice president of football operations, Ernie Accorsi, gave Bernie the ultimate compliment when he said: "Mentally, Kosar is like [Hall of Fame quarterback] John Unitas. They have that gunfighter's stare, both of them. They command the respect of their teammates without ever opening their mouths."

A year later, in 1987, Bernie proved his past season was no fluke. Nineteen eighty-seven was the year of the players' strike, so Bernie played in just 12 games, but he brought the team another AFC Central title. He completed 62 percent of his passes, while throwing for 3,033 yards, with 22 touchdowns and 9 interceptions. His 95.4 quarterback rating was the best in the AFC. Once again he had the lowest interception rate in the entire league, and he was named to the Pro Bowl for the first time.

Then came the playoffs, and he was brilliant once again. First he threw for a 38–21 win over Indianapolis, which set up a rematch for the AFC championship against the Denver Broncos.

Once again it was a matchup between Kosar and Elway. The Broncos dominated the first half, as Elway led them to a 21–3 advantage. In the second half, Bernie Kosar caught fire and threw two touchdown passes. Byner then scored another on the ground. Denver still held a 31–24 lead. But then Bernie moved his team 86 yards on nine plays, throwing to Slaughter from the four for the score. The kick tied the game at 31–31.

Unfortunately, it was still the Broncos who came out on top. Elway led a drive resulting in the go-ahead score, making it 38–31. Bernie then drove the

Browns again. From the eight, he gave the ball to Byner, who circled left. He was headed for the tying touchdown when he was stripped of the ball at the three. Denver recovered. Seconds later they took an intentional safety to get a free kick. Time ran out and the Broncos won, 38–33.

But Bernie had shown his stuff once more. He had hit on 26 of 41 passes for 356 yards and 3 scores. More impressive were the 16 of 22 passes he completed in the second half alone, good for 256 yards and all three TDs. It was an amazing performance, and if it hadn't been for the fumble, he could have had his club in the Super Bowl.

In 1988 the team made the playoffs again as a wild card, at 10–6. But it was a season that saw Bernie getting hit more often as age and injuries took their tolls on his offensive line. In fact, he missed seven regular-season starts and the wild-card playoff game with injuries. He still completed 60.2 percent of his passes and threw for 1,890 yards. But the competitor in him hated to miss those games.

"Bernie hates to lose," said teammate Brian Brennan. "Even at golf. I remember him shooting a 77 in a pressure game at Shaker Heights. Ever see his golf swing? It's the ugliest thing in the world. But it's accurate."

Just like his passing. The problem, however, was the pounding he was taking. The Browns won the AFC Central Division in 1989 with a 9-6-1 record under new coach Bud Carson. Bernie was the fourth-leading quarterback in the conference, completing 303 of 513 passes for 3,533 yards and 18 scores. But he played through elbow pain, dislocated right index and middle fingers, a strained shoulder, and, during the

This is a typical Kosar pose. His sidearm throwing style and follow through is not supposed to work in the NFL. But Bernie has been outstanding since his rookie year with the Browns and has produced many brilliant performances. *(Vernon J. Biever Photo)*

playoffs, a staph infection that swelled his right arm to almost double its normal size. He was sacked 34 times.

"With injuries," said Bernie, "a lot of it is whether you think you're hurt. I just don't think about injuries."

Once again the Browns lost the AFC title game to Denver, this time by a 37–21 count. Bernie was just 19 of 44 for 210 yards, with two TDs and three interceptions. Everyone knew he was hurting. One story said that Bernie's throwing arm and hand "were held together by glue, baling wire, bandages, and a rubber band." Under the circumstances, he did extremely well.

But in 1990, more people began worrying about his health. Former NFL quarterback Archie Manning said what a lot of people were thinking: "I'm very worried about Bernie. The pass rushers are so much bigger and more mobile than when I played. He's taking worse hits than I ever did."

But Bernie remained philosophical. "I don't think about my future," he said. "I think it's best to think week to week."

It turned out to be a losing season for the Browns, yet Bernie was the second best quarterback in the AFC, behind Jim Kelly of Buffalo. He threw for more than 3,000 yards and once again had the lowest interception percentage in the league.

A year later, with new coach Bill Belichick taking more pains to protect his quarterback, Bernie really proved that he was one of the most accurate passers of his generation. He did not suffer an interception in the first 308 passes he threw that year. That was a new NFL record. The former record holder was the great Bart Starr, who was a Hall of Famer with the Green Bay Packers in the 1960s. Starr's mark was 294 passes without an interception.

"To go this long without an interception in the NFL, with all the great defensive talent out there, you've got to have some breaks," said Bernie. "And for us to be competitive, I just can't afford to make mistakes."

Others saw the feat as more than luck. Bernie still had perhaps the greatest feel for the passing game of all the quarterbacks and great accuracy in throwing the football.

The Browns didn't make the playoffs that year, though Bernie was again outstanding. Nor did they make it in 1992. Bernie missed a good part of that year with a broken ankle. He missed 10 weeks, then in the final game of the season he broke the ankle in the same spot.

After the season had ended, he had surgery on the ankle. Two screws were set in it to help the healing process. Doctors anticipate a complete recovery. The Browns will need the skills and daring of Bernie Kosar to get back in the playoff hunt.

"Our goals haven't changed," Bernie said. "Our goal is still to win the Super Bowl."

Prior to the 1990 season, the Browns rewarded Bernie with a new six-year contract worth some $15.3 million. They have seen what he can do in big games and over the course of a season. If he can stay healthy, he may get a chance to win the big one yet.

WARREN MOON

WHAT ARE THE ODDS OF A QUARTERBACK THROWING for more yards than any professional signal caller in history and still having to prove himself? Sounds impossible, doesn't it? But it actually comes close to describing the situation Warren Moon found himself in prior to the 1992 season.

Moon is the strong-armed, veteran quarterback who commands the high-scoring, run-and-shoot offense of the Houston Oilers. He has led the Oilers into the NFL playoffs for six straight years, beginning in 1987. In 1991, Warren set single season records for the most passes attempted and most completed. He has now thrown for more than 51,000 yards in his pro career, which began back in 1978.

Why then is Warren Moon still not considered to be one of the great quarterbacks in NFL history? For beginners, Warren didn't enter the National Football League right after completing his career at the University of Washington. NFL scouts didn't rate him as a

Warren Moon has traveled an unusual road to stardom. It took him from the University of Washington to the Edmonton Eskimos of the Canadian Football League and finally to the Houston Oilers of the NFL. *(Courtesy Houston Oilers)*

top prospect. Also he felt that a black quarterback might not get a full shot at running a team.

So instead of the NFL, Warren Moon went to Canada and set the Canadian League on fire. He led his team, the Edmonton Eskimos, to five straight Grey Cup championships, which is the Canadian equivalent of the Super Bowl. By that time, the NFL had changed its mind about Warren Moon and was ready to welcome him with open arms.

Warren joined the Oilers in 1984. Three years later he helped put them into the playoffs and has kept them there ever since. He is recognized today as one of the top players at his position—except for one thing. He hasn't led the Oilers to the Super Bowl, which, unfortunately, has become the measuring stick for quarterbacks.

So Warren Moon continues his quest, despite a 1992 season ender that no fan will ever forget. Warren would never make an excuse, though. He's not that kind of guy. In fact, he's probably one of the most respected athletes in the Houston area, an exceptional man in many ways. Whenever Warren Moon has had to prove himself, he has.

Harold Warren Moon was born November 18, 1956, in Los Angeles, California. He and his six sisters were mainly raised by their mother, Pat. His father died when Warren was just seven, which made it difficult for the family. But they stuck together and persevered.

Mrs. Moon was a nurse but couldn't always work because of her young children. Warren remembers that the family always had the essentials and never really wanted for anything.

"My mother has definitely been the most influential person in my life," Warren has said. "She did so much with so little and kept everything in line around the house. She sacrificed a lot for us, and I always said that if I got into a position to help her, I would."

As a young boy, Warren gravitated toward sports. His first football experience came with the Baldwin Hill Trojans, in the Pop Warner Football League. He performed with and against future NFL stars Wendell Tyler, Butch Johnson, and James Lofton. His coaches recognized his talent and encouraged him by working with him. Quite early he showed the drive and desire to be the best player he could, one who was willing to make sacrifices to achieve his goals.

At Hamilton High School in Los Angeles Warren

was a three-year letterman as a quarterback. By his senior year he was close to his full height of 6'3" and headed for 200 pounds. He was fast and had a strong throwing arm.

As a high-school senior he was exceptional. He had a number of great games, but his best passing effort was a 16-for-23 performance, good for 289 yards and a pair of touchdowns. When the season ended he was not only an All-City performer but an All-American as well. Yet there was not a flood of college recruiters banging down his door. It must have been disappointing to him.

Part of the reason could have been the relatively small number of black quarterbacks at that time. Because he wasn't heavily recruited, Warren decided to attend West Los Angeles Junior College his freshman year. Not surprisingly, he had a fine season there and finally some major colleges began to recruit him.

Warren had to consider what his future would be as he was recruited. He was aware that his chances of playing in the National Football League as a quarterback weren't great. Many black quarterbacks were looked on as athletes rather than signal callers. In fact, at that time there had not been a single black NFL quarterback who could be called a major star.

Warren's first choice of a college might have been the University of Southern California, but Vince Evans was already established as the quarterback there. Coincidentally, Evans is also black.

Warren chose to go to the University of Washington, despite the fact that only some 3.5 percent of the student body was black. The Huskies played in the PAC-8 Conference, so Warren would get to compete against California schools—USC, UCLA, Stanford, and California. And when he won the starting quarterback job as a sophomore, it appeared that things couldn't be better.

Things aren't always what they appear. Many Washington fans didn't want Warren as quarterback. At first he was booed, and along with the boos came many racial slurs. His girlfriend, Felicia, who later became his wife, was upset listening to the names that Warren was being called. It weighed heavily on Warren's mind.

"It was difficult for me because I was only 18 years old," he said. "And it was the first time I had been away from home. There were a couple of times when I thought about giving up, but my mother told me that I had never quit anything before. So I followed her suggestion to stay there, stick it out, and make the best of it. But those experiences taught me an awful lot about people."

Warren didn't have a great year as a sophomore. He started the first six games, then played in spots after that. He completed only 48 of 122 passes for 587 yards. The Huskies finished at 6-5.

A year later he was back and better. This time he started all 11 games and began to do the things expected of a future pro. Washington didn't rely on a heavy passing game. Warren handed off to his backs, and when he threw, it was strictly as a drop-back passer. So the Huskies didn't take full advantage of his athletic talents.

Still, he had a better year, throwing for 1,106 yards by completing 81 of 175 attempts. His passing percentage was up to 46.3, and he tossed for six touchdowns, with eight interceptions.

Warren's best day came against Stanford, when he

completed 15 of 28 passes for 209 yards and two TDs. Against Washington State in the season finale, he connected on touchdown passes of 40 and 45 yards. At this point he still wasn't being talked about as a hot pro prospect, and the team finished a mediocre 5-6. So much of his football future seemed to hinge on his senior season of 1977.

It was apparent right from the start that Warren was better than ever in 1977. At 6'3" and 205 pounds he was big, strong, and tough enough to hang in the pocket. His passing accuracy had improved and the Huskies began letting him throw more. He had also evolved into a leader, and one with a winning team.

Warren had a number of big games that year, and when the regular season ended the Huskies were 10-2 and PAC-8 champions. In addition, Warren Moon was the PAC-8 Player of the Year. He completed 113 of 199 throws for 1,584 yards and 11 touchdowns. He was intercepted just seven times and also ran the ball 99 times for 266 yards and scored six more TDs on the ground. So his numbers were up, including his completion percentage, which was now a very respectable 56.8.

He capped his Washington career by leading the Huskies to a 27–20 upset over Michigan in the Rose Bowl on New Year's Day, 1978. He was named the Most Valuable Player in that game. It would seem that he would now be considered one of the quarterback elite. But that still wasn't the case.

Warren saw some of the NFL scouting reports. The consensus was that he was no better than a fourth-round pick. Fourth-round picks don't usually get very good contracts. He also wondered if he'd get a real chance to show his stuff, especially if he was drafted as a backup quarterback.

He went over his options carefully and decided to play for the Edmonton Eskimos of the Canadian Football League. He was never even drafted by an NFL team. As far as the NFL and its fans were concerned, he didn't exist.

But that was far from the case in Canada. Warren quickly showed that his talents were suited to the Canadian brand of football. The Canadian game has some fundamental differences from its American counterpart. It's a wide-open game played on a field that is ten yards longer and also wider than the American gridiron. The end zones are 25 yards deep instead of the 10 in the American game, and a team has three downs to make 15 yards for a first down, instead of four downs to make 10 yards.

That makes Canadian football a quick-strike game. And that's just what Warren Moon brought to the Eskimos: the ability to strike fast and strike often. The Eskimos under Coach Hugh Campbell had a solid team when Warren arrived in 1978, so Campbell decided not to start Warren but to bring him in when the team needed a change of pace.

It worked perfectly. Warren didn't start a game for three years, yet his playing time continued to increase.

His first season the Eskimos finished with a 12-4-2 record and went on to win the Grey Cup, the trophy given to the winner of the championship game. For the year, Warren completed 89 of 173 passes for 1,112 yards, five touchdowns, and seven interceptions. His completion percentage was 57.4.

With Warren seeing more and more action, the Eskimos won five consecutive Grey Cups through 1982, an incredible achievement in any professional sport. Coach Campbell said that Warren Moon played a big role in his team's success.

"For six straight years Warren took his team as far as it could go and then won the big game," Campbell said. "He did it his final year at Washington, winning the PAC-8 and the Rose Bowl. Then five straight years here. That should tell you something about the man."

Warren's numbers also continued to get better until they reached almost unbelievable proportions. His second year he threw for 2,382 yards, then hit 3,127 his third and 3,959 his fourth. That year, 1981, he started 9 games, completed 62.7 percent of his passes, and threw for 27 touchdowns with just 12 interceptions. He also ran for 298 yards on 50 carries.

But it was in 1982 that he really exploded. A full-time starter that year, he completed 333 passes in 562 attempts for an even 5,000 yards. That made him the first quarterback in any professional football league to throw for 5,000 yards in one season. He also had 36 touchdown passes that season, with only 16 interceptions.

The Eskimos' run of championships ended in 1983. The team finished at .500, but no one could fault Warren Moon. He put together perhaps the greatest season of any quarterback in the history of the game. He was absolutely brilliant from start to finish that year.

When the season ended he had completed 380 of 664 passes for an amazing 5,648 yards. That is still the most passing yards for any quarterback in the history of football. He also threw for 31 touchdowns with only 19 interceptions. But that wasn't all. He ran the ball 85 times for a team-leading 527 yards, an average of 6.2 yards per carry. That means he accounted for more than 6,000 yards in total offense by himself.

Needless to say, Warren was the winner of the Schenley Award, given to the CFL's Most Valuable Player. In six years of CFL play he had done it all. It was now time to head south and play in the National Football League.

He might have been virtually neglected by the NFL back in 1978, but now all 28 teams expressed interest in him. What he wanted was a team that could best utilize his talents.

He was concerned, though, that there were still very few black quarterbacks in the NFL. There were no starters in 1983. He talked to a pair of black former NFL signal callers, Doug Williams and James Harris. Both felt he should come to the NFL.

Finally Warren and his agent made a list of the eight teams they felt could best utilize his talents. He wanted to do it right so he began to travel around, visiting the teams and the cities in which they played. He wanted the right situation for himself, his wife, and two children. He remembered what had happened to him his first year at the University of Washington. Because of that, he didn't want to be in a place where he felt the fans would turn on him if he wasn't immediately successful.

The teams he considered were the Seahawks, Saints, Raiders, Bucs, Giants, Eagles, Colts, and Oilers.

"I know ultimately that I'll have to constantly prove myself on the field," said Warren. "But I know that I can compete and do well in the NFL. All I want is a real opportunity to show what I can do."

Perhaps the thing that finally swayed him was the announcement that the Houston Oilers had hired Hugh Campbell as their coach for the 1984 season. Campbell had been Warren's coach for all six years in Edmonton. If anyone knew Warren's talents and how best to utilize them, it was Hugh Campbell.

It came down to a choice between Seattle and Houston. Warren lived in Seattle in the off-season, and the Seahawks had just come off their best season ever. They had gone all the way to the AFC title game before losing to the Raiders, 31–14. The Oilers, meanwhile, seemed to be floundering and had a long way to go to get back in contention.

In 1983, several QBs split the top job. Oliver Luck was the best of a mediocre group. If Warren played in Houston, there was little doubt that he would be the immediate number one. But with a bad team, even the number-one man can look bad, not to mention the beating he might take.

Finally on February 3, 1984, Warren made the announcement the football world was waiting for. He would sign a pact with the Houston Oilers, a contract that would pay him some six million dollars over the next five years. It would make him one of the highest paid players in the sport.

"One reason I chose the Oilers is because I was determined to go where I was wanted. Houston showed me that they wanted me. When I was here two weeks ago I was introduced at a [Houston] Rockets game and the fans gave me a tremendous ovation that made me feel very warm inside. And I also came to Houston because I like challenges."

113

Coach Campbell was delighted to be reunited with Warren Moon. He knew that quarterback was one position he wouldn't have to worry about.

"If I had to talk about Warren's shortcomings [as a quarterback], it would be a very short talk," said Campbell.

The Oilers thought of Warren as the player who would lead them back to respectability. Since 1978, the leader of their offense had been the great running back Earl Campbell. Campbell had gained 1,450 yards as a rookie and two years later rushed for 1,934 yards. Already one of the great ones, Campbell had still gained 1,301 yards on 322 carries in 1983. But he would be injured in '84, and after that he would leave the Oilers.

So Warren would not have the benefit of a great running back. His Oilers' debut came against the Raiders, and he went 12 for 29 for 201 yards and 2 scores. But the Oilers lost, 24–14. A week later he opened it up and gave the fans a glimpse of the future. Throwing passes all over the field, Warren had the Oilers' offense moving. He completed 23 of 43 for 365 yards, but the team lost again, this time to the Indianapolis Colts, 35–21.

That would set the pattern for the entire year. Warren moved the team and produced some outstanding games. Respect around the league for Warren was growing quickly.

Despite Warren's passing exploits, the Oilers lost their first ten games. They then won three of their final six. Warren was 19 of 26 in a 17–16 victory over Kansas City, then hit 20 of 28 for 207 yards and three touchdowns in a 31–20 win over the Jets. He also led

In his first year with the Oilers, Warren showed poise and savvy. He was quick enough to scramble away from defenders, then used his strong arm to connect with his receivers downfield.

(Vernon J. Biever Photo)

the club to a win over the Rams. But a 3-13 finish left the Oilers in last place.

When the year ended, Warren had completed 259 of 450 passes for 3,338 yards. He'd completed 57.6 percent of his passes and thrown 12 touchdowns with 14 interceptions. Not surprisingly, he was named to every All-Rookie Team. Some rookie. Warren was already 28 years old and had been one of the great quarterbacks in Canadian Football History.

It would be three frustrating seasons before the Oilers began to turn things around. Warren's second season was especially frustrating. The team was on the way to a 5-11 finish. Warren wasn't having as strong a season as he had in '84, missing two games with a hip pointer. But the real bad part came after the 14th game, when Coach Campbell was suddenly fired and replaced by the colorful Jerry Glanville. Warren felt he had lost a friend.

"That was the lowest point of my career," he said. "When Coach Campbell was fired I felt I had been lied to. I'd been told that he would have an opportunity to rebuild. I began to feel that I didn't fit in. I didn't feel that I was being used right. It was frustrating."

Glanville had been the defensive coordinator under Coach Campbell, and when he got the head job he continued to concentrate on building a powerful defense. One of Warren's main gripes was that he had three different quarterback coaches his first three years. The system and the philosophy kept changing.

In each of his first three years he threw more interceptions than touchdowns. The 1986 season was another 5-11 year. Three straight losing seasons. That was something Warren wasn't used to, especially after a 1-8 start, which led him to criticize Glanville for the first time. Warren said there were too many running plays.

"Coach Glanville called me in and said I should have spoken to him first," explained Warren. "He said from now on we would open up on offense. Of course, we were already 1-8 and out of it. But we did open up the offense and won four of our last seven games."

In 1987 he had more tools to work with. Mike Rozier was a good, solid running back. Wide receiver Drew Hill had joined the team in 1985, followed by Ernest Givens in '86. In 1987 rookie wideouts Curtis Duncan and Haywood Jeffries joined the team. All were quick, elusive receivers who could catch the football.

June Jones, a former NFL signal caller, was the new quarterback coach, and he began to put in some run-and-shoot plays in which Warren would sprint out and look for one of his four wide receivers. Slowly the team began to win.

In the 1987 season the team won three of its last four to finish at 9-6 and make the playoffs as a wild-card team. The team would be in its first playoff game in seven years, meeting the Seattle Seahawks.

Warren had an outstanding game and had the Oilers in front, 13–10, at the half. It was 20–13 after three, but Seattle tied it in the fourth quarter. Then in overtime, Warren drove the Oilers into field-goal range and Tony Zendejas booted a 42-yarder to win it. Warren was 21 of 32 for 273 yards and a score. Next the team would be meeting Denver in the AFC divisional game.

This wasn't as close. It was 24–3, Denver, at the

half and a 34–10 final. Warren passed for 264 yards in a losing cause. But he and his teammates felt they were starting to build and all looked forward to 1988.

In the season opener at Indianapolis, Warren was hit hard in the third period and suffered a fracture of his right shoulder blade. The team won the game, 17–14, and the next day Warren was put on injured reserve for five weeks. Rookie Cody Carlson took over and played well enough to help the Oilers win three of their next five games.

Warren returned to lead the club to a 34–14 victory over Pittsburgh and took it from there. He had some big games the second half of the year as the Oilers finished at 10–6, good for second place in the AFC Central and a spot in the playoffs as a wild card once again.

The team won a squeaker over Cleveland, 24–23, in the wild-card game but then lost a 17–10 decision to a good Buffalo team in the next round. But they had made the playoffs two straight years and Warren Moon had his finest season.

Despite missing 5 full games, Warren hit on 160 of 294 passes for 2,327 yards, 17 touchdowns, and just 8 interceptions. His quarterback rating of 88.4 was his best ever and fifth best in the entire NFL. He also helped the Oilers become the second highest scoring team in the NFL, with 424 points. For his efforts, he was an honorable mention All-Pro and selected to play in his first Pro Bowl.

It seemed that 1989 was another step forward. The Oilers had again made the playoffs with a 10-6 record, and Warren had another "best" year, accounting for 3,631 yards, completing 60.3 percent of his passes, and throwing for 23 touchdowns. A 26–23 loss to the Steelers in the wild-card game was a disappointment.

Yet after the season he was named *Football News* AFC Player of the Year, UPI First Team All-AFC, and garnered another Pro Bowl appearance. He was also named the NFL's Traveler's Man of the Year for outstanding off-field community work.

But there were problems that surfaced after the season ended. It was reported that a coolness had developed between Coach Glanville and Warren. Glanville never criticized Warren in public because he knew his quarterback was one of the most popular athletes in the Houston area. The Jaycees named Warren one of the Five Outstanding Young Men of Texas. He did a great deal of charity work, and when his church in Houston, the Windsor Village Methodist, needed $200,000 to complete a community center, it was Warren Moon who donated the entire amount! Not many athletes or many people would do that.

On the football front, the team had yet another quarterback coach in 1989. Kevin Gilbride had coached a run-and-shoot type offense in the Canadian League, so he and Warren were on the same wavelength. But Warren felt that Glanville took over on game day and didn't stick to the offensive game plan.

"Jerry's system was to let June and then Kevin handle the concept, the offensive game plan," Warren said. "He would let them do all the work during the week, and then on Sunday, Jerry would take over the play calling. It was done by instinct."

Being diplomatic, Warren didn't air his grievances until after a coaching change was made. Glanville was dismissed and Jack Pardee became the new coach. Pardee had coached at the University of Houston, where he used the run-and-shoot exclusively, which was the offense he wanted for the Oilers.

Before the 1990 season started, the coaches told Warren that he had better keep his arm in shape because he was going to throw perhaps more than any other quarterback in history. He was also told to be prepared to run a variety of sprint outs, to read defenses, and to be ready to get hit.

"I'm going to be 33 in November," Warren said shortly after the new season began, "so I'm in the winding-down stage of my career. How long that stage lasts, I don't know. I'm definitely playing some of my best football right now. To me, being in your prime means playing your best and feeling your best, too.

"I can see things on the field I couldn't see when I was younger, but physically, I can see myself slowing down. I still have pretty good escapability, but once I turn upfield, I don't move as quickly."

No one would ever guess Warren was slowing down by the way he started. In the opening game, at Atlanta, he hit on 31 of 52 passes for 397 yards and four touchdowns. The only problem was that the Oilers lost, 47–27. Now that the offense was cooking, had the defense fallen behind?

Warren's numbers continued to be outstanding. Using his four fine wide receivers on nearly every play, he pulled the trigger on the run-and-shoot as perhaps no other quarterback had. He was racking up big yardage totals. The second week it was 284, then 308, 355, 191, 369, 202, and 381. At midseason the Oilers were just 4-4, but Warren Moon was on a pace that would bring him close to the NFL record for completions, attempts, and passing yards. Everyone had a favorite Moon throw to talk about.

Against the New York Jets, he threw a nine-yard touchdown pass to Haywood Jeffries while backing up on his heels. The throw was all arm, but the ball whistled to its target. Later in the same game he ran to his left and fired a perfect pass to Drew Hill 40 yards downfield. The ball was on target—but dropped.

"I have faith in this offense," said Warren. "I know we can move the ball consistently. We just have to take that step upward."

Warren felt he still wasn't considered in the same class as Joe Montana, John Elway, Jim Kelly, or Dan Marino. And that's where he wanted to be.

"I'm used to it [the lack of recognition] by now," he said. "But somehow I never seem to be spoken of in the same breath with the really top names in the game. Hopefully, there's still time."

Warren continued to throw the football. In the 14th week, against Kansas City, he went wild, completing 27 of 45 passes for a whopping 527 yards, the second most in NFL history. The Oilers won that game, 27–10.

After it was over, Sid Gillman, who had coached in the NFL for years and was recognized as an offensive genius, said this about Warren Moon: "I think he's great, not good but great. He could be the best ever. I've never seen a better exhibition of throwing the football than in his performance against Kansas City, and I've seen a lot of football games in my lifetime."

Unfortunately for Warren, his season would end the following week, in game 15. He had already thrown for 288 yards against Cincinnati when late in the fourth quarter he hit his throwing hand on the helmet of an onrushing Bengals' lineman and suffered an open dislocation of his thumb.

The Oilers won their final game and made the play-offs. But the following week they were beaten by Cincinnati, 41–14, to end their season once more.

As for Warren, he had completed 362 of 584 passes for 4,689 yards, a 62.0 percent completion mark, 33 touchdowns, and just 13 interceptions. His quarterback rating was a career-best 96.8. He had produced a truly superstar season. He led the NFL in completions, attempts, and yardage. He tied Dan Marino's record with nine 300-yard passing games. His four wide receivers each caught more than 65 passes, the first time that had happened in the history of the league.

Then came the individual honors. Warren made the Pro Bowl, he was named AP Offensive Player of the Year, he finished second in the Miller Lite NFL Player of the Year voting, he was a *Sporting News* first-team All-Pro. It went on and on. There was no doubt about Warren's ability and talent now.

He then went out and repeated his heroics in 1991. This time the team was 11-5, as Warren started all 16 games. He set a new NFL record for attempts, with 655, and completions, with 404. He was again first in passing yards, with 4,690. That made him the third QB in history to post back-to-back 4,000-yard seasons. Against the Jets he completed 41 of 56 passes, the second most completions ever in a single game. The numbers just kept coming.

For the fifth year in a row, the Oilers were in the playoffs. First came a wild-card victory over the Jets,

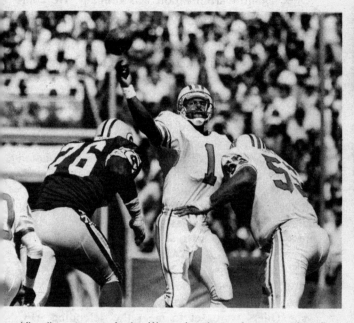

Like all great quarterbacks, Warren has the toughness to wait until the last second to throw the football, even if it means taking some big hits. He has led the Oilers to the playoffs six years in a row.

(Vernon J. Biever Photo)

Bill Gutman

17–10, which put the club in the divisional game with the Broncos.

Once again Warren Moon was brilliant. He completed 27 of 36 passes for 325 yards and 3 scores. He had his team ahead, 21-6, at the half. But the Broncos chipped away at the lead. With 2:07 left, the Oilers held just a 24–23 advantage. The kickoff was downed at the Denver two-yard line.

They fell victim once more to another John Elway miracle finish. The Bronco quarterback drove his team deep into Houston territory with some clutch passing. With 16 seconds left, the ball was at the 11-yard line. David Treadwell then came on and booted a 28-yard field goal to give the Broncos the victory and send the Oilers home again.

It seemed as if the Oilers just couldn't get over that final hurdle. The 1992 season was no different, as the Oilers went on to a sixth straight trip to the playoffs.

Warren wound up the AFC's best passer, completing 224 of 346 passes for 2,521 yards and a 64.7 completion percentage, a career best. He threw for 18 scores with 12 interceptions.

The Oilers were set to meet the defending AFC champion Buffalo Bills in the wild-card game. In the first half Warren was absolutely brilliant. In the first quarter he led an 80-yard drive, highlighted by a 32-yard pass to Haywood Jeffries. With the ball at the three, he cranked up and hit Jeffries in the end zone for the first score.

Buffalo made it 7–3 before the quarter ended. But in the second period Warren really went to work. Another 80-yard drive resulted in a seven-yard TD toss to Webster Slaughter. Then a 67-yard drive ended when Warren hit Curtis Duncan from 26 yards

124

out. And finally he drove his club another 67 yards and threw a 27-yard bull's-eye to Jeffries for yet another touchdown. At the half the Oilers held a seemingly insurmountable 28–3 lead, Warren having connected on 19 of 22 passes for 218 yards and four touchdowns.

Then, early in the third period, Oiler defensive back Bubba McDowell intercepted a Frank Reich pass and returned it 58 yards for yet another Houston score. That made it 35–3, and for all intents and purposes the game seemed over. But then something changed.

Frank Reich, the Bills' backup quarterback, started to find the mark and the momentum turned. Reich led the Bills to four third-quarter touchdowns, three on passes, to cut the lead to 35–31. No one could believe what was happening. Then midway through the fourth quarter, Reich drove the Bills 74 yards and finished it with a 17-yard scoring pass to Andre Reed. Incredibly, the Bills had taken the lead, 38–35.

Warren knew the game was on the line and drove his club 63 yards on 12 plays, allowing Al Del Greco to kick the tying field goal with just 15 seconds left. The game then went into overtime. That was when Warren made a mistake. On a third and three from his own 27, he tried to hit Jeffries. But the throw was wide and Buffalo intercepted. A face-mask penalty against Houston after the interception moved the ball to the Houston 20.

Three plays later Steve Christie kicked a 32-yard field goal to give Buffalo the greatest come-from-behind win (32 points down) in National Football League history. The Oilers couldn't believe what had happened. Most of the players left the field in a state of shock.

Warren just sat in the trainers' room for half an hour, total disbelief on his face.

"All I've been doing is just sitting there trying to figure the whole thing out," he said finally. "I just don't believe it happened, but I guess it did."

Warren had completed 36 of 50 passes for 371 yards and 4 scores. But it was the interception of his final pass that led to the game winner.

Six straight years in the playoffs and still no ring. For Warren Moon it had to be a terrible disappointment. Because like all great players, Warren Moon dearly wants an NFL championship. He knows time may be running short. But as Warren said years earlier, when he thought about leaving the University of Washington, "I had never quit anything before."

Houston fans should know that he won't quit now.

TROY AIKMAN

HE'S BIG AND STRONG WITH A CANNON FOR A THROW-ing arm and the nerve of a riverboat gambler. Put him at the helm of the Dallas Cowboys, *America's Team,* and the result should read—Superstar!

But for Troy Aikman it hasn't been easy. His first high-school team was simply awful. In college he was a passing quarterback on a team that loved the wishbone formation. That's like mixing oil and water.

In the NFL his team had a new owner, a new coach, and a total rebuilding program, which often means the quarterback is sacrificed. These were some of the circumstances under which Troy Aikman has played quarterback.

As a collegian, Troy changed his situation. He went from the University of Oklahoma to the University of California at Los Angeles (UCLA), the result being that he became a consensus All-American. Aikman had the last laugh.

Now he's had it as a pro, too. For in four short

Troy Aikman's boyish features sometimes hide the tough competitor he has always been. Once he puts on his pads and helmet, his only objective is to win the game.

(Courtesy Dallas Cowboys)

years, the Dallas Cowboys have gone from a 1-15 laughingstock team to Super Bowl champions. America's Team is back and Troy Aikman's at the helm, performing the way everyone expected him to when he joined the team in 1989.

But Troy Aikman isn't looking for a last laugh or an I-told-you-so. He just wants to do his job and do it well. He is very happy to leave the limelight to others.

This shy and self-effacing superstar was born Troy Kenneth Aikman in West Covina, California, on November 21, 1966. He spent his early years in Cerritos, a small town just east of Los Angeles, with his father, mother, and two sisters.

Like many top athletes, young Troy took to sports early and easily. He played football, basketball, and baseball and was good at all three. He liked living in California and had a lot of friends.

When he was 12 it all changed. One day Mr. Aikman told the family they were moving to Oklahoma, where he would be working. So Troy suddenly went from a sprawling suburb of Los Angeles to Henryetta, a small Oklahoma town of 6,000 people.

"I hated it," he said. "I just couldn't understand why we moved there. My friends were in California and I was already doing well in sports there."

But kids usually adapt quickly. "Within a couple of months it felt like I had lived there my whole life," he said.

The only problem came when he reached Henryetta High and had to play football for the mediocre Fighting Hens. The team was so bad, in fact, that Troy wasn't even thinking about playing college football. In Troy's junior year as starting quarterback, the Hens lost their first eight games. Same old Henryetta.

But then the team surprised everyone. They won their final two games to finish the year at 2-8. That qualified them for the state tournament, since there were only four teams in the conference. Though they lost in the first round, it was considered a successful season.

The next year everyone had a new attitude and commitment. With Troy again at the helm, the team put forth an even greater effort and finished the year at 6-4, which was like winning the Super Bowl.

Troy was already 6'3" and weighed over 200

pounds. He earned 10 letters at Henryetta, then had to decide where to go in the fall of 1984. There were not a lot of big-time college recruiters after him. Troy quickly made a verbal commitment to go to Oklahoma State University.

But he also visited the University of Oklahoma. Oklahoma was big-time, bigger than Oklahoma State, and the Sooners were often a national power. The problem was that they used the wishbone formation, in which passing is usually secondary.

When Troy spoke with Oklahoma coach Barry Switzer he was told that the Sooners were in the process of changing from the wishbone to the I-formation, and that they would be throwing the ball more.

"Deep down I wanted to believe they were going to throw the football," said Troy. "I wanted to believe it so badly that I ended up going there."

Troy said that none of the recruits communicated much during visits to the school or maybe things would have been different.

"Everybody was always saying that he [Coach Switzer] changed the offense for me," Troy said, "but that's simply not true. He changed the wishbone a little bit, but the only real difference when I played was that we threw the ball twelve times a game instead of seven."

If it sounds as if it's adding up to a not-so-happy experience, that's true. Despite his size, strength, and great throwing arm, Troy was relegated to third string and never expected to play as a freshman.

Oklahoma had its usual outstanding team in 1984 and was 5-0-1 after six games. Then, a few days before the Kansas game, it was determined that starting quarterback Danny Bradley couldn't play because of an injury. The backup signal caller was declared academically ineligible. Suddenly an unprepared Troy Aikman was thrust into action.

The game was a disaster. The Sooners lost, 28–11, and the fingers of blame pointed straight at Troy.

"The Kansas game shattered my confidence," Troy admitted. "It was very hard to come back my sophomore year and hear people saying I was going to be benched if I didn't have a great game."

Troy was played very sparingly the rest of the year. The Sooners ended up the sixth best team in the country, according to the AP poll. Some felt the club had a chance to be number one the following year, and Troy returned to try again. He won the starting job in the preseason, beating out Jamelle Holieway.

The Sooners won their first three games with Troy at the helm. He had completed 21 of 40 passes for 317 yards, not the big numbers a real passing offense would produce, but better than the usual Oklahoma fare. In fact, against Kansas State he hit on 10 of 14 for 177 yards. There was no doubt about his potential. But it also became apparent that Coach Switzer wasn't entirely comfortable compromising on the wishbone to accommodate Troy's passing. Before game four, against powerful Miami, the coach decided to change things a bit.

"They told me not to be upset if they brought Jamelle in on third downs for a little more speed," Troy said. "But I was upset."

That's because a third down is traditionally a passing down, and the Oklahoma coaching staff was turning away from Troy. No wonder it bugged him.

Troy started, and for the first time since he had

131

come to Oklahoma he was on top of his game. He was throwing with poise and authority, completing six of his first seven passes for 131 yards and a touchdown. But then in the second quarter he was tackled hard and didn't get up. He was helped from the field, his left ankle broken and his season over.

Oklahoma lost to Miami, but with Holieway at the helm and the wishbone back in place, the Sooners ripped through the rest of their schedule. And when they defeated Penn State in the Orange Bowl, 25–10, they were declared national champions.

Troy watched that game standing on the sideline on crutches. "I think we still would have won the national championship with me playing," he said.

The wishbone had been so successful that in the spring of 1986 Coach Switzer wasted no time in naming Holieway his starter for the fall season. Troy could stick it out and hope for a chance to play somewhere down the line. But he couldn't build a career waiting for another guy to get hurt.

The other option, of course, was to transfer. That would mean going to another school, sitting out a year, then playing his final two seasons. He decided that was best.

Coach Switzer helped Troy by making several phone calls. One of them was to UCLA coach Terry Donahue. Switzer told Donahue that Troy was an outstanding passer who would be an NFL first-round draft choice someday.

"I really knew nothing about Troy Aikman then," Coach Donahue said. "But I figured Barry had had enough number-one picks to know what one looked like. So I said we'd be interested."

UCLA offered Troy a scholarship, and he went

there in the fall of 1986 and began to work out with the Bruins' squad.

"When I saw him move around, I finally began to get excited," said Coach Donahue. "That's when I began to feel we had gotten something special."

Troy was redshirted in 1986, meaning he practiced with the team but didn't dress for games. He would still have two years of eligibility remaining. It didn't take Coach Donahue long to decide that Troy would be his quarterback in 1987 instead of the returning Brendan McCracken. The Bruins built their offense around Troy's strong right arm, and the strategy paid immediate dividends.

In the opener, against San Diego State, he hit 8 of 10 passes for 166 yards. That was just the beginning. Pretty soon, the big games began to come—his biggest against Arizona State. Showing poise and ability, he connected on 22 of 31 passes for 328 yards. The accolades began to flow in.

"Figures validate that Aikman . . . is the most efficient quarterback in the land," said Bob Hurt, a reporter with the *Arizona Republic*. "A pro personnel director told me last week that Aikman would be the first player picked in a draft a year from now. This guy has it. He has size. He has vision. He has poise."

There was one big disappointment in 1987. The game with archrival USC took place on November 21, Troy's 21st birthday, and it was one of those days all athletes dread. He completed just 11 of 26 passes for 171 yards. Worse yet, he threw three interceptions after throwing just three in the previous 10 games. The Bruins lost, 17–13.

"It was probably the worst day of my life," Troy said. "I never really got in a groove, never felt comfortable throwing the football. I couldn't sleep for two weeks after that game. I just kept playing every play over and over in my head.''

He bounced back to lead the Bruins to a victory over Florida in the Aloha Bowl, giving them a 10-2 record. Troy's numbers were incredible. He completed 178 of 273 passes for 2,527 yards, 17 touchdowns, and just eight interceptions. His completion percentage was a gaudy 65.2. Those were NFL-like numbers.

Needless to say, he made a number of All-American teams and was named PAC-10 Offensive Player of the Year. In the eyes of almost everyone, he was the number-one pro prospect in the land.

The 1988 season turned into almost a carbon copy of 1987, except that Troy was a year older and a year better. He again led the Bruins to a 10-2 season. He completed 228 of 354 passes for 2,771 yards, with 24 touchdowns and just nine interceptions. His completion percentage was 64.4.

He ended his college career by leading the Bruins past Arkansas in the Cotton Bowl, enabling UCLA to win a bowl game for the seventh consecutive year, an NCAA record. He was a consensus All-American and he finished third in the balloting for the Heisman Trophy. It was also a foregone conclusion that he would be the first of the collegiate quarterbacks taken in the 1989 NFL draft.

The team that had the first pick in the draft was the Dallas Cowboys. Early in 1989 the Cowboys were in the process of writing the biggest story in sports. In February it was announced that the team had been sold to Jerry Jones, a highly successful businessman from Arkansas. When he purchased the team, he was

After transferring to UCLA from Oklahoma, Troy became an immediate All-American. He led the Bruins to a pair of winning seasons
before becoming the number-one draft choice of the entire National Football League.

(Courtesy the University of California at Los Angeles)

immediately looked on with suspicion by native Texans, who considered him an outsider.

Jones's first big move was to fire Tom Landry, who had been the only coach the Cowboys ever had. Landry was an institution in Dallas. Jones quickly announced that the new coach would be Jimmy Johnson, the collegiate coach from the University of Miami and an old friend and teammate of Jones's. But Jones had not simply hired one of his buddies—he had hired the man he considered the best coach in the country.

Jones and Johnson knew that the only way they could prove themselves was to make the Cowboys the best organization in football. They started out to do that from day one. One of the first orders of business was to use their draft choices wisely.

Coach Johnson headed out to UCLA to put Troy Aikman through a predraft workout. After watching Troy go through several passing drills, Johnson rushed to a phone booth and called Jerry Jones. He was so excited he began shouting into the mouthpiece. Jones remembers his words.

"Jimmy kept yelling, 'We've got our quarterback, we've got our quarterback,' " Jones said.

Jerry Jones and Jimmy Johnson were convinced and opened negotiations immediately. Even before draft day they had signed Troy to a six-year contract worth some eleven million dollars, a record for an NFL rookie. A short time later they officially made him the first pick in the entire draft.

Now it was a matter of who would win the number-one job. Troy wasn't an automatic shoo-in. In the supplemental draft, held some time later, the Cowboys tabbed Miami quarterback Steve Walsh, who had played under Johnson. So Walsh and Aikman would be competing for the number-one job.

Troy was the starter in the first preseason game of 1989, completing 8 of 11 throws, one of them for a score. Offensive coordinator David Shula was pleased.

"He picked up blitzes. He audibled well. He was good and calm, and I was impressed," said Shula.

Walsh didn't play well in his quarter of action, but Coach Johnson gave the impression that the job was still up for grabs.

"This is not a formality," he said. "They know they'll get an equal chance. Steve will start next week's game, and then we'll be better prepared to make a decision."

Both quarterbacks were 6'3". But Troy weighed 220 pounds to 195 for Walsh. It was generally acknowledged that Troy had the stronger arm and was the better all-around athlete.

Jerry Jones continued to talk as if Aikman were the main man.

"Troy Aikman helps restore the Cowboy image," the owner said. "He's got this winning aura. I can't help smiling when he so much as jogs from one practice field to the other."

Troy had to work long and hard to learn the Cowboys' playbook. He said there were some things about the pro game that made passing more difficult than it had been in college.

"Defensive backs can disguise their intentions more easily in the pros," he said. "Because the hash marks are narrower, the ball is always closer to the middle of the field. So if you're a defensive back you can wait a lot longer before committing to a certain part of the field.

"In college, I was making a lot of presnap reads. Here the quarterback has to read defenses as he drops back. So it was much easier in college."

Troy was finally named the starter before the first regular-season game. The Cowboys visited the New Orleans Saints and took a pasting. The final was 28–0. The team was full of weaknesses. Troy was picked off twice. During the preseason he had thrown 63 passes without an interception.

The Cowboys had one of the top running backs in the game in Herschel Walker. In 1988 Walker ran for 1,514 yards, but in this opener with New Orleans, Walker gained just 10 yards on eight carries.

"We've got a long way to go," was all Coach Johnson said.

The next week the team blew a 21–10 halftime lead at Atlanta and lost, 27–21. Troy was 13 of 23 for 241 yards in that one, throwing his first TD pass, a 65-yarder to second-year wideout Michael Irvin. But the next week he hit just 6 of 21 for 83 yards as the club lost to Washington, 30–7. Rookies will have days like that.

Then came the game against the New York Giants, when Troy fractured his left index finger and had to come out. Estimates were he'd be lost to the team for four to six weeks. Now Steve Walsh would get his turn.

On October 12, the Cowboys shocked the football community by trading Herschel Walker to the Minnesota Vikings for five players, six conditional draft choices, and a 1992 first-round pick. The Cowboys wound up with the best of the deal, though it would take several years to reap the rewards.

While Troy was still out the team won its first game, a 13–3 decision over Washington. A week later Troy returned in a big way. He threw for 379 yards and two scores against Phoenix, but the Cowboys lost anyway, 24–20. But no other NFL quarterback threw for more yards that week.

The team was now 1-9 and it wouldn't get any better. The Cowboys finished the year at 1-15, the worst record in their history. Many fans longed for the days when Tom Landry always had the team in the playoffs.

Troy ended the season with 155 completions on 292 attempts for 1,749 yards, nine touchdowns, and 18 interceptions. His completion percentage was 53.1, but his quarterback rating of 55.9 was last among qualifiers in the NFC. It made him think twice about the future.

"There were times when I was beginning to wonder if I wanted to continue playing pro football," Troy said. "When you go all year without winning a single game it's a tough thing to take."

Coach Johnson and owner Jones were extremely busy during the off-season. They made a number of trades and signed some 16 Plan-B free agents. Then they drafted Emmitt Smith, a running back out of Florida, on the first round. In early September they traded Steve Walsh to New Orleans for a first and third draft choice in 1991 and a conditional second pick in 1992.

That deal accomplished two things. It enabled the Cowboys to stockpile draft choices with which to build the team, and it told Troy Aikman that he was definitely the quarterback around whom they would build an offense. Troy realized that things were going to get better and had already put the last season behind him.

In the 1990 opener, Troy quarterbacked his first victory as the Cowboys topped San Diego, 17–14. He was only 13 of 29 for 193 yards, but delivered when it counted. He connected on six of nine passes for 68 yards in the fourth quarter and scored the winning touchdown on a one-yard plunge with just 1:58 left on the clock.

A week later Troy and his teammates realized it could still be difficult. They lost to the Giants, 28–7. The defensive-minded New Yorkers completely stifled the Cowboys' attack. The team then lost six of its next eight and were struggling again at 3-7.

After a bad loss to San Francisco in which Troy threw for just 96 yards, he suddenly exploded against the Rams. Pulling out all the stops, he threw for 303 yards and three scores, hitting on 17 of 32 passes as the Cowboys stopped a three-game slide and won, 24–21. Better yet, he led an 89-yard drive in the fourth quarter to set up the winning field goal.

"Aikman is coming of age," read one scouting report. And in the next three weeks he continued to prove it. He threw for 222 yards in a win over Washington, hit 71.4 percent of his passes (15 of 21) in a victory over New Orleans, and then connected on 12 of 18 as the Cowboys won their fourth straight, topping Phoenix. The team was suddenly 7-7 with an outside shot at the playoffs.

Against the Redskins, Troy led the team on a pair of long fourth-quarter drives resulting in the touchdowns that won the game, 27–17. In the New Orleans game he completed 11 straight passes in the second half while engineering a pair of fourth-quarter drives that gave Dallas a 17–13 victory. So it wasn't only that he was winning, it was the *way* he was winning.

His value to the Cowboys could be seen in the final two games. After throwing one pass against the Eagles he sustained a shoulder injury and missed the rest of the game, as well as the finale with Atlanta a week later. Dallas lost both to finish at 7-9, but it was a great improvement over the 1-15 mark a year earlier.

Coach Johnson was especially happy the way his young quarterback was developing, and all the trades, draft choices, and Plan-B signings were paying off.

"We've made significant improvement," said the coach. "We have a realistic shot at winning almost every time we go on the field now and these players believe they can win."

Troy finished the season with 226 completions on 399 attempts for 2,579 yards and a 56.6 completion percentage. He threw for 11 scores and had 18 picked off. His quarterback rating was up from 55.7 his rookie year to 66.6. His development seemed right on schedule.

In 1991 Troy Aikman and the Cowboys came of age. Troy set the theme in the opener against Cleveland, when he completed 24 of 37 passes for 274 yards and two scores. The Cowboys won, 26–14. A couple of losses followed, a close one against Washington and then a shutout at the hands of Philadelphia. The Philly game was Troy's poorest of the year. After that, he began to catch fire.

The team won four straight, and in the second of those victories, Troy went on a four-game streak that

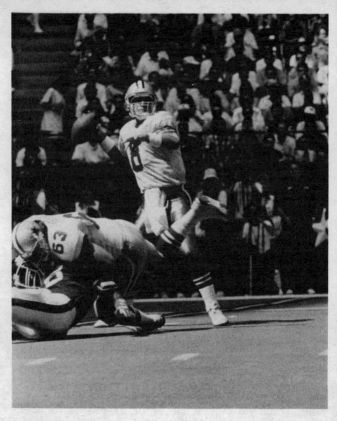

At Dallas, Troy endured a 1-15 season as a rookie. Just three years later, however, he quarterbacked the Cowboys to a great Super Bowl victory. He is widely considered the best of the new generation of NFL signal callers. *(Courtesy Dallas Cowboys)*

saw him pass for 277, 287, 276, and 331 yards. His completion percentage in those games was close to 70 percent. He was leading the NFC in completions and yardage and seemed on his way to setting a number of team records.

Although Troy continued to play well, the team suffered a letdown and dropped three of their next four. The team was 6-5 and about to meet division rival Washington once more. Troy was playing very well against the Skins and by the third quarter he had completed 13 of 20 passes for 204 yards and had his team in front, 14–7. Then he was hit hard and came up limping. He had to leave the game. Steve Beuerlein came on to complete a 24–21 Dallas win.

The diagnosis was strained ligaments. Troy would miss the final four games of the season. Beuerlein took over, and while he didn't have the numbers Troy had rung up, the Cowboys did win their final four games to finish at 11-5 and nail down a wild-card playoff berth.

Beuerlein's late-season heroics partly overshadowed the great season Troy Aikman had had. Playing in 11 games and a little over half of a 12th, he completed 237 of 363 passes for 2,754 yards and a completion percentage of 65.3. He threw for 11 touchdowns with 10 interceptions and had a fine quarterback rating of 86.7. His passing percentage led the NFC and he was named to play in his first Pro Bowl.

But the Cowboys had to enter the playoffs without their top quarterback. Beuerlein led them to a victory over the Bears in the wild-card game, 17–13. Then came the divisional game against the Detroit Lions. That was when the bubble finally burst. The Lions won easily, 38–6, ending the Cowboys' season. It had been, however, a highly successful year. Just two seasons after going 1-15, the team was back in the playoffs at 11-5.

Though Beuerlein did a fine job in a relief role, there was little doubt that a healthy Troy Aikman was still the main man.

"Aikman proved in 1991 that he is already among the quarterback elite in the league," said one assistant coach. "And everyone who has seen him feels he can only get better. He has the talent to become an all-time great."

Coach Johnson was happy with his team's finish in 1991, but he was looking for even more. Having tasted a national championship at Miami, the coach knew there was only one ultimate goal in the NFL— winning the Super Bowl. He and owner Jones continued working to get the best players to balance out the team. Perhaps the most important pickup early in the 1992 season was defensive lineman Charles Haley, who had already been part of a Super Bowl team in San Francisco.

It turned out to be a brilliant season for the Cowboys, one reminiscent of the old days. They blasted foe after foe, doing it with a combination of offense and defense, a deep and balanced team. Troy was close to brilliant all year. He had become an efficient and deadly quarterback, slicing up defenses with precision passing and nerves of steel. The offense now had complete confidence in him.

Smith continued to be the premiere running back in the league, while Irvin was among the top receivers. He was complemented by the speedy Alvin Harper and the continued fine play of tight end Jay Novacek. A massive offensive line gave Troy outstanding protection as well as opened up holes for the elusive Smith.

When the season ended, the Cowboys had a 13-3 record and had reclaimed the NFC Eastern Division title. Only the San Francisco 49ers, at 14-2, had a better record. This time the Cowboys were one of the favorites in the playoffs, though the consensus was that the 49ers were still the best overall team in either division.

Troy had his best season yet. He completed 302 of 473 attempts for an NFC-best 3,445 yards. He threw for 23 touchdowns and had just 14 intercepted, completing 63.8 percent of his passes. His quarterback rating was 89.5, ranking him third in the NFC. Now it was time for the playoffs.

The Cowboys played host to their division rivals the Philadelphia Eagles in the divisional game. The Eagles were a physical, punishing, defensive team that had a potentially explosive offense, led by Randall Cunningham. Many felt the Philadelphians would stop the Cowboys. But the Dallas defense, without a Pro Bowler, was the top-ranked in the NFC.

The game was close in the first period. Philly scored first on a 32-yard field goal by Roger Ruzek. But toward the end of the quarter, Troy drove the Cowboys 46 yards on 10 plays, tossing a one-yard TD pass to tight end Derek Tennell. The kick made it 7-3. Then in the second quarter, Dallas and Troy Aikman began to open it up. They drove 67 yards in just five plays, the key being a beautiful 41-yard hookup between Troy and Alvin Harper. A six-yard Aikman-to-Novacek TD toss ended the drive. It was now 14-3.

Troy had looked a little shaky early in the game,

missing seven of his first 10 passes. After the second score he said he had settled down.

"I was having a hard time getting a grip on the ball early," he said. "It was slipping out of my hands. Someone said I was too pumped up, but that wasn't the case. That 41-yard bomb to Alvin Harper lifted my confidence. Plus our defense forced two turnovers early and gave us great field position."

After that the rout was on. It was 17–3 at the half and 34–3 before the Eagles scored a late touchdown to make the final 34–10. The Cowboys had advanced to the NFC title game against the powerful 49ers.

Troy wound up completing 15 of 25 for 200 yards and two scores. Smith gained 114 yards rushing and Irvin caught six passes for 88 yards.

Even though the 49ers were favored, the Cowboy players felt they could win. The game was played at Candlestick Park in San Francisco on a slow and wet field. The Niners were quarterbacked by lefty Steve Young, who had been the league's top passer. If anyone could outplay Troy, it might be Young.

Like the Eagles game, this one was close at the beginning. Dallas scored first on a field goal, then the Niners came back, Young running it over from the one. San Francisco had a 7–3 lead at the end of the quarter. In the second period the Cowboys recovered a fumble and went 39 yards for the go-ahead score, Smith running it over from the five. But a San Francisco field goal before halftime made it a 10–10 deadlock at intermission. The game was still up for grabs.

Troy started the second half by taking his club 78 yards in eight plays. On one play Troy made a last-second read and dumped a quick pass to Irvin, who converted it into a 16-yard gain. Then on the next play he showed his touch by lofting a deep pass down the right sideline to Harper, who outjumped the Niner defender and gained 38 yards to the seven. Two plays later the Cowboys ran it in for the go-ahead score. It was 17–10.

A Niner field goal made it 17–13, but the Cowboys weren't about to lose momentum. This time they went 79 yards on a classic drive that took nine minutes and brought them into the fourth quarter. Troy completed seven of eight passes on the drive, eating up 70 yards. A 16-yard pass from Troy to Emmitt Smith took it into the end zone. The kick made it 24–13.

The Niners came back to score and close the gap to 24–20. That was when Troy and the Cowboys showed their poise once more. With just over four minutes left, Troy hit Alvin Harper on a slant and the speedy receiver turned it into a 70-yard gain. That was the back breaker. The TD came on a six-yard pass from Troy to Kelvin Martin. Even though the extra point was missed, the TD made it 30–20 and that was the way it ended. The Cowboys were headed to the Super Bowl.

Troy had been brilliant. He finished with 24 of 34 for 322 yards and two scores. In the second half alone he was 13 of 16 for 208 yards. He had plenty of help, especially from Emmitt Smith, who went over 100 yards again. Now it was on to the Rose Bowl in Pasadena, California, the scene for many of Troy's college triumphs, where the Cowboys would be meeting the AFC Champion Buffalo Bills.

The Bills had lost the two previous Super Bowls, and while the Cowboys were one-touchdown favorites, Buffalo was the popular choice. Many felt the

Bills would finally put it together and win. And when a blocked punt early in the game led to a Buffalo touchdown and a 7–0 lead, it looked as if the Bills might do it.

But it wasn't long before the tempo of the game changed. Dallas didn't move the ball its first couple of possessions, and Troy admitted later he was a bit tight.

"I had to talk myself into relaxing," he said.

Then Buffalo made its first mistake. Quarterback Jim Kelly tried to hit tight end Pete Metzallaars. But Metzallaars slipped and the ball was picked off by James Washington. Troy then drove the Cowboys 47 yards on six plays. The touchdown came on a 23-yard pass to tight end Jay Novacek. The kick tied the game at 7–7 with less than two minutes remaining in the quarter.

That set the pattern. Buffalo kept turning the ball over and the Cowboys took advantage. The offensive trio of Troy, Emmitt Smith, and Michael Irvin all shone, with plenty of help from the rest of the Cowboys. On Buffalo's first play from scrimmage following the Dallas TD, quarterback Kelly was hit by defensive end Charles Haley. The ball popped into the air and Dallas's Jimmie Jones grabbed it and fell into the end zone for another score.

That opened the floodgates. After a Buffalo field goal, Troy hit Irvin on a 19-yard scoring pass to finish a 72-yard drive. And right before the half he connected with Irvin again, this time from 18 yards out, to make it 28–10. At the half Troy had hit on 14 of 19 passes for 148 yards and 3 scores. He was putting on a super show.

It was more of the same in the second half. Buffalo

continued to self-destruct with turnovers and Aikman continued to play brilliantly. It was a 31–17 game after three quarters. Then early in the fourth period, Troy connected with Alvin Harper from 45 yards away for the touchdown that really put it away. An Emmitt Smith touchdown run and fumble recovery by linebacker Ken Norton, Jr., completed the scoring.

The Cowboys had won the game, 52–17, and were world champions!

It had been an incredible run for the Cowboys and for Troy Aikman. They went from a 1-15 disaster in 1989 to a Super Bowl title in three years. Troy finished the game with 22 completions on 30 attempts for 273 yards and four touchdowns. He was the overwhelming choice as the game's Most Valuable Player.

Like all the Cowboys, Troy was ecstatic after the game. "This means everything to me," he said. "A tremendous weight is off my shoulders. No matter what happens, I can say I took a team to the Super Bowl and won it."

As of 1992 Dallas was the youngest team in the league. Their talent is awesome. Their coach is singularly dedicated to winning. And arguably they've got the best young quarterback in the National Football League. In the eyes of many, Troy Aikman is really *that* good.

About the Author

BILL GUTMAN has been an avid sports fan ever since he can remember. A freelance writer for twenty-one years, he has done profiles and bios of many of today's sports heroes. Mr. Gutman has written about all of the major sports and some lesser ones as well. In addition to profiles and bios, he has also written sports instructional books and sports fiction. He is the author of Archway's *Sports Illustrated* series; *Bo Jackson: A Biography; Michael Jordan: A Biography;* and *Great Sports Upsets,* available from Archway Paperbacks. Currently, he lives in Poughquag, New York, with his wife, two stepchildren, and a variety of pets.